Arianna Snow's
Novels

The Lochmoor Glen Series

Visit the
Golden Horse Ltd.
website:

www.ariannaghnovels.com

Watch for the sixth in the series!

"*Patience, My Dear*, a superbly authored tale.
My Magic Square, must-read sequel, a
delicious pleasure from beginning to end."

—Midwest Book Review

𝕭𝖑𝖊𝖘𝖘𝖊𝖉 𝕻𝖊𝖙𝖆𝖑𝖘

A NOVEL

Arianna Snow

Golden Horse Ltd.
Cedar Rapids, Iowa

This book is primarily a book of fiction. Names, characters, places and incidents are either products of the author's imagination or actual historic places and events which have been used fictitiously for historical reference as noted.

An *Original Publication of Golden Horse Ltd.*
P.O. Box 1002
Cedar Rapids, IA 52406-1002 U.S.A.
www.ariannaghnovels.com
ISBN 10: 0-9772308-4-8
ISBN 13: 9780977230846

Library of Congress Control Number: 2008925183
First Printing
Volume 5 of The Lochmoor Glen Series

Printed and bound in the United States of America
by Publishers' Graphics, LLC

Cover: Design by Arianna Snow
        Photography by EZ
        Keys by londonjoiners.com
        Layout by CEZ
        Printed by White Oak Printing, Lancaster, PA

♥

In memory
of
our beautiful
black lab

Angel Patience

"Angie Face, Honey Baby I love you"

My Special thanks to:
God

my husband
everything

KAE, CE, LC
editorial

my babies, grandbabies, relatives and friends
support

My loving parents, DD, KAE
for bookkeeping and packaging

LC
word processing
♥

HIRAM GEOFFREY MCDONNALLY FAMILY TREE

PATERNAL GRANDPARENTS
CAPTAIN GEOFFREY EDWARD MCDONNALLY
CATHERINE NORTON MCDONNALLY

FATHER
CAPTAIN GEOFFREY LACHLAN MCDONNALLY

UNCLE
EDWARD CALEB MCDONNALLY

MATERNAL GRANDPARENTS
ALEXANDER THOMAS SELRACH
SARAH GLASGOW SELRACH

MOTHER
AMANDA SELRACH MCDONNALLY

SISTER
HANNAH RUTH MCDONNALLY

NIECE
SOPHIA MCDONNALLY

CARETAKERS
ALBERT ZIGMANN
ELOISE ZIGMANN

SON - GUILLAUME ZIGMANN

FRIENDS
DANIEL O'LEARDON
ABIGAIL O'LEARDON

RAHZVON SIERZIK

NAOMI BEATRICE (MACKENZIE) MCDONNALLY FAMILY TREE

PATERNAL GRANDPARENTS
JEREMIAH NORMAN MACKENZIE
OCTAVIA HILL MACKENZIE

FATHER
NATHAN ELIAS MACKENZIE
DAGMAR ARNOLDSON MACKENZIE (STEPMOTHER)

MATERNAL GRANDPARENTS
JAMES HENRY SMITHFIELD
IRENE CLEBOURNE SMITHFIELD

MOTHER
BEATRICE SMITHFIELD MACKENZIE

BROTHER
JEREMIAH JAMES MACKENZIE

DAUGHTER
ALLISON SARAH O'CONNOR

HUSBAND
EDWARD CALEB MCDONNALLY

FRIENDS
HARRIET DUGAN
JOSEPH DUGAN
HENRY MCTAVISH

The Chapters

Chapter 1

"Silver Lining"

"Here at my feet
what wonders pass,
What endless,
active life is here!"

—Matthew Arnold

The morning was quiet at Brachney Hall. Edward and Naomi enjoyed the simple breakfast that Eloise had prepared for them. They were finishing the last few bites of porridge and baps when Edward patted his mouth with his napkin. "Excellent meal."

"Yes, and to think she has a delicious carrot cake in the oven," Naomi added.

"We really need a cook, Naomi, or I shall be forced to lure Eloise away from Hiram with large sums of money," he joked.

"I highly doubt that there is enough money in the world to separate her from the McDonnally cottage. There is a little matter of her husband in Hiram's employ, as well."

"Albert can come, too. I can use another hand around here. It would lighten the load for Angus and his crew."

"Edward McDonnally, I do believe you are serious."

"Nearly, but maybe the Zigmanns know of someone we could hire. All of my prospects fell through. I never thought to ask Eloise."

"With all the commotion with Hiram, the kidnapping and your ladder escapade, there has not been time for talk of much else, Edward."

"Please ask Eloise, the next time you see her, love. Were you not planning to see her this morning?"

"Is this not a ploy to have me fetch a piece of carrot cake for you?" Naomi asked with suspicion.

"I would run the errand myself, but being a poor soul with battered limbs and confined to this chair, it may be rather tasking," he said pathetically.

"Oh, I do not know about that. It may be invigorating for you to wheel yourself down the road for dessert."

"Now love, you know how arduous it is to move this contraption across the cobblestones," Edward whined.

"Do not think you are fooling me for one minute, Mr. McDonnally. I know what you have in mind—you want to dispose of me, so you can lose yourself in the Zane Gray novel that Hiram gave you."

"No, that could not be further from the truth, *Mrs. Holmes*."

"Very well, I will not be gone long." She leaned over Edward who had pulled his wheeled chair away from the dining room table. "I hope you will not be bored." Naomi raised a suspicious brow and kissed him on the forehead.

"Not to worry, love." Edward smiled, eyeing the book on the table across the room. Naomi walked casually over, picked up the western novel and thumbed through it. Edward's smile disappeared with concern.

"I think Albert would enjoy this," she commented nonchalantly and started to leave the room with it.

"*Naomi.*"

She ignored Edward's warning and continued to the hall, while he wheeled frantically after her.

"Bring my book back!"

He turned into the hall where Naomi stood snickering, hidden behind the loaded coat tree.

"I confess—you were right!" he called out to the seemingly empty hall.

Naomi stepped forward, giggling, "No white lies with me, Edward Caleb!" she forewarned and surrendered the book to him.

"Very well, but I *was* in the middle of a very exciting chapter."

Naomi reached down and ruffled his hair like he was a mischievous little boy. A moment later, Heidi, her little dachshund, appeared in the hall, dragging something fifty times her size.

Alarmed at the sight, Edward scolded the pup, "Blast you, dog!"

"What is it?" Naomi asked, bending down to examine the beautiful, large quilt.

Edward scowled with fury as he noticed a number of "chewed" holes in the once perfect coverlet.

"Edward, I have not seen this in any of the bedrooms." Naomi admired the professional stitching. "I am so sorry. Heidi, you naughty dog!"

Naomi struggled to fold the cumbersome quilt, while examining the delicate patterns. She paused with perplexity when she spotted a familiar picture woven in one of the squares—a man lying under a cart. She began unfolding it quickly to find another square depicting a picnic basket by a pond. Her eyes widened when she saw the embroidered square of numerals. She slowly turned to Edward who sat downcast next to her.

"Oh Edward, it is the most splendid example of handwork that I have ever seen."

Edward remained silent, fighting with all his masculinity to hold back his angry tears of disappointment.

Naomi knelt down beside him. "I truly love it.... I can repair it. It is the most thoughtful—"

She stopped, seeing his devastation. Edward could not speak. His wedding surprise had been destroyed in every sense of the word. Naomi squeezed his hand, now limp of emotion. Recognizing that no words could relieve his pain, she stood up, folded the quilt, and carried it into the dining room. She placed it at the end of the table and returned to the hall where she found Edward dejected and staring blankly. She put on her wrap and placed a second kiss on his forehead.

"I will fetch the cake, love. I will be back soon. Come along, Heidi."

Naomi closed the door behind her and moved mechanically toward the road with Heidi at her heels. The pup followed tail down, aware of Naomi's disapproval. Naomi stopped at the corner of the house. *My poor, dear Edward.* She wanted to run back to comfort him, but her own disappointment forced her on; a special moment from their wedding day was lost, never to be replaced. To make matters worse, she knew that her limited ability in quilting would never permit her to restore the gift to its original, superb condition. Even had she been qualified, she felt that there was something so wrong and unnatural in repairing one's own wedding gift. She looked down with disgust at her canine companion and abandoned her destination to continue along the side of the house to the flagstone path leading to the pond. In seeing the spot where she and Edward enjoyed their first picnic outing, another pang of disappointment shot through her body.

Numb with frustration, Naomi sat down, beneath the tree. Heidi immediately jumped on her lap and attempted to make amends by licking Naomi's tears. Naomi pushed her aside.

"Go on, leave me alone. You are a bad girl. I do not want to see you."

The confused little dog sat next to Naomi, wagging its tail, then darted off into the grass towards the end of the pond.

Naomi's thoughts of self-pity ended abruptly with Heidi's incessant barking in the distance.

"Oh be quiet, I am in no mood to play!"

Heidi ran back to Naomi as fast as her short legs could carry her and then barked three times beckoning her to follow.

"No, Heidi, no."

Heidi returned to the grassy tuft at the end of the pond and howled pathetically.

"All right," Naomi left her pouting position to assist the demanding pet. She finally reached the spot where Heidi stood anxiously. Naomi looked down, threw her hands up in horror and screamed.

"It cannot be! Mr. Kilvert said that he *found* your body." She leaned down to look closer.

"But it *is* you."

She knelt down beside the near lifeless, little form. "My poor little baby," she lifted it and cradled it in her arms. "What has happened to you? Where have you been?" she said tearfully, examining the matted, dirty coat. Naomi stood up and started running up the flagstone path.

"Come on, Heidi. Edward! Edward!" she screamed.

Edward, seeing Naomi at the window of the door, wheeled madly to meet her.

"By George, can it—it cannot be!" Edward said in awe.

"Yes, Edward, yes! It is my Patience and she is still alive!"

"Wrap her in a towel—she is shivering. Put her on my lap and go to Eloise. Jump to it, love!"

"Edward! Forget your blasted dessert!"

"No, Naomi! Eloise has medical training—we need her."

"Yes, yes, what am I thinking?" Naomi turned to leave and nearly stepped on Heidi, blocking the doorway.

"Move, Heidi." Naomi looked down to slip past when she noticed a small mewing miniature standing innocently next to the dachshund. "What on earth? Edward, Edward look there is another one!" Edward repositioned his chair to see the new arrival. The tiny kitten rubbed against the protective dog and gave a slight meow.

"Where did *that* come from?" Edward asked in surprise.

Naomi picked up the kitten and cuddled it. "I think it is Patience's baby," Naomi deduced.

Edward looked at the kitten, then the old cat skeptically.

"Naomi, put it up on my lap with Patience and get going."

"I will be right back." she gave Heidi a loving pat and sped off to McDonnally Manor. Edward sat stroking Patience, and encouraged the battered cat in a calm soothing tone.

"Hold on, little lassie, hold on for Naomi." The tiny offspring curled up next to its *mother* and fell peacefully asleep.

Naomi darted out of the front door and sped on foot towards the woods. At the end of the long trek, she saw Mr. Kilvert, on horseback, leaving the drive at McDonnally Manor.

"Mr. Kilvert, Mr. Kilvert!"

"Mrs. McDonnally?" The postman halted his horse and turned.

"Mr. Kilvert, Patience, my cat— she is alive!"

"What?"

"Yes, it is her." Naomi caught her breath as she arrived by his side. "The cat you found must have belonged to some other poor soul. My Patience is alive—I would know her anywhere. However, she appears ill. If you will excuse me, I need to find Eloise."

"Well, be on yer way, lassie. I'm happy for ya!"

Running to the mansion door, Naomi turned and called out, "Mr. Kilvert, Patience has a baby!" Mr. Kilvert smiled curiously and waved with approval. Naomi disappeared behind the large entry door to Hiram's home and called down the hall.

"Eloise, Eloise!"

"In the study, mum!"

Naomi entered through the pocket doors. The housekeeper sat at the small writing desk with her lace ribbon, which Daniel had carried in his wallet for years, draped across the palm of her right hand. She looked up at Naomi's flushed face, closed her hand discreetly around the ribbon and stood. Naomi was momentarily distracted by the housekeeper's downcast demeanor.

Eloise asked, "What is it, mum?"

"Eloise, have you been crying?"

"It is of no consequence, now. What troubles you, mum?"

Naomi grasped Eloise's shoulders. "Eloise, you will not believe this—Patience is back!"

"Patience?"

"Yes, but she is ill. We need you to look her over, please come with me to Brachney Hall."

Eloise stuffed the lace ribbon into her apron pocket and quickly followed Naomi outside. The two women took the wagon back to Brachney Hall where they entered to find Edward sitting in his chair with the two cats. Eloise hurried over to the ailing pet.

"My, my, I thought I had seen the back of you, Miss Patience. I shan't believe it. What is *this*, Naomi?"

"I was so excited; I forgot to tell you about this one. The kitten was with her."

Eloise shook her head, laid Patience on the towel spread on the table and placed her ear on the cat's back.

"Her breathing is clear. She seems to be exhausted, and a little dehydrated. Keep her covered and prepare her some warm milk and porridge. As much as you vexed me, I am glad to see you, you belligerent beast." She stroked Patience's forehead. "You look atrocious. You need some brushing and a great deal of rest. We will know by this evening how she fairs. I cannot believe it," Eloise shook her head. "Take care of her, mum. I never thought that I would pray for a cat, but this is an exception." The cat squinted with apparent appreciation. "I wonder what my Rusty is going to think of this. Well, I shall be going now; I have a cake in need of icing." Edward's head rose with interest.

"Thank you, Eloise." Naomi walked her to the door.

"Yes, Eloise, thank you. You are a jolly good physician! I should like to sample that cake!" Edward called.

On her return ride to the manor, Eloise's thoughts fell back to the lace ribbon, which she had found wedged in the book in her master's study.

"Daniel, dear Daniel," she murmured, while passing the woods dividing the estates. "I truly hope that you find someone to love."

At Brachney Hall, Naomi and Edward followed Mrs. Zigmann's instructions, then prepared a bed for the cat in the laundry basket. Patience opened her eyes several times, seemingly checking out the whereabouts of her youngster. The tiny kitten spent no time in joining its mother by pulling its body up the side of the basket with its front claws, to leap inside. It curled up next to Patience and dozed off. Heidi peered over the edge with front paws resting on the top rim of the basket. She nearly tipped the basket over twice before Naomi scolded her and sent her to lie on a blanket next to the basket. Edward and Naomi returned to the dining room, leaving the pets to rest quietly.

Edward wheeled next to the rocking chair by the window where Naomi sat. "It has been quite a day, love."

"You know, Edward, it is all very strange."

"Patience's return?"

"Yes, the entire sequence of events. I thought about it on the return with Eloise. Edward, I do not want to make excuses for Heidi's ill behavior with the quilt, but had she not damaged it and brought it to us, I would have never left to the pond. Heidi may not have found Patience in time."

"The silver lining theory?"

"Perhaps. I believe that sometimes God finds it necessary for us to make a sacrifice to carry out his plans."

Edward smiled. "A quilt for a cat."

"Patches for Patience." Naomi suggested. "What do you think we should call our newest edition?"

"Patches?" Edward suggested.

"No, I think that our finding him was simply destiny, so... "Destiny".

"*Destiny* for a male, Naomi?"

Naomi frowned disapprovingly at his criticism.

"Naomi, maybe we should drop the 'tiny', that would be discouraging for the little guy. Why not just Dest?"

Naomi thought for a minute, "Dest? Hmm? Very well, Dest."

"Now about that dessert, Naomi...should you not be going?"

"'Twill all be well: no need of are;
Though how it will, and when, and where,
We cannot see, and can't declare."

—Arthur Hugh Clough

Chapter 11

"Permission"

"Like the angel of life,
   Too kind to depart,
You hang on my lips,
   You hang on my heart!"

—John Hall Wheelock

Following the evening meal in the dining room of McDonnally Manor, Hiram sat with his niece, Sophia, and his friend Daniel. Seated on his right, was Abigail, the woman Hiram loved.

"Daniel, may I have a word with you in the study?" Hiram asked with an air of mystery.

Abigail immediately reached under the table and squeezed Sophia's wrist. Sophia turned to her in confirmation.

Yes, Abigail, you are about to become officially engaged to my uncle, she thought, sharing her friend's anticipation.

"Today, Hiram? I am feeling a bit tuckered out." Daniel yawned beneath his hand. Abigail glared in disapproval.

Hiram wiped his mouth with his napkin. "Aye, perhaps I should probably turn in early tonight. It has been a tasking day."

"*Daniel,*" Abigail warned through clenched teeth.

"Now, Abby, ye heard what the man said; he is ready to turn in."

"But, *Daniel,*" Abigail looked to him in alarm.

"I hear tell Naomi found her cat." Daniel changed the subject.

"*Dear brother,*" Abigail said impatiently.

"Perhaps, I could work a chat into me schedule, if me friend is up to it." Daniel grinned.

Her attention directed quickly to Hiram.

Hiram hesitated, too, enjoying Abigail's intense aggravation. "Very well," he stood up, "shall we go to the study?" he asked without concern.

Daniel placed his napkin on the table and addressed Eloise, who was clearing the dishes on to the tray. "A lovely meal, Eloise."

"Thank you, Mr. O'Leardon."

"Eloise, please bring Daniel a cup of coffee and tea for me," Hiram instructed.

"Yes, sir."

Hiram playfully squeezed Abigail's shoulder as he passed. Thoroughly pleased with their performances, Daniel and Hiram intentionally left the room in lackadaisical stride.

Hiram slid open the door to the study for Daniel and followed him in. He walked to the fireplace where he offered Daniel a chair and the two men took their respective places across from each other. Hiram postponed addressing the purpose of the meeting and began the conversation with an inquiry to Daniel's return trip to Lochmoor Glen.

"How was your trip from London, Daniel? I understand that it was actually quite eventful."

"Aye, I see that me young friend, Ahab— *Rahzvon* seems to be quite fond of our Sophia," Daniel noted.

"Aye, Rahzvon is a good lad. His father would be proud of him. He is a hard worker and an honest young man."

"I was a wee leery of leavin' him with Sophia, but seems to have turned ou' for the best."

"Initially, I had my doubts about his character, as well." Hiram leaned back and crossed his ankles. "I know *one* who was not too pleased with his arrival. Young McTavish has had his eye on Sophia."

"McTavish?" Daniel questioned.

"The sailor, who has made a home with the Dugans."

"Ah, I remember, ya mentioned he had a riff with Guillaume o'er Allison." Daniel looked toward the shelves and left his chair to search for the volume where he left Eloise's ribbon bookmarked between the pages. Daniel located the book and pulled it from the shelf, left of the fireplace.

"Daniel, where did you meet Rahzvon?"

"We found him behind me cousin Rupert's cottage in Manchester."

"Ah, you and your cousin found him."

"Nay," Daniel replied reluctantly and carried the book back to the chair.

"Who then?" Hiram asked suspiciously.

Daniel remained focused on the book as he quickly flipped through the pages in search of the memorable piece of ribbon.

"Daniel?"

"A woman."

Hiram shot up in his chair. "A woman?"

Daniel looked up. "Is it so inconceivable to think o' *me* with a woman?" he asked defensively.

"Of course not, I only assumed that you and Rahzvon were traveling alone."

Daniel looked down at the book with a perturbed expression.

"An elderly woman?" Hiram asked gently.

"Nay!" Daniel slammed the book closed, disturbed in finding the ribbon to be missing. *Ellie must have found it,* he thought.

"Easy, man. I meant no harm."

Eloise's knocking interrupted their conversation. She entered at Hiram's invitation.

"Your drinks, sir."

"Thank you, Eloise."

She carried the teacups, jiggling in the saucers and stared nervously at Daniel holding the *book.*

"Eloise, let me help you," Hiram offered as he reached for the coffee cup. Eloise unexpectedly thrust the teacup towards him. The collision resulted in both cups crashing to the floor. The trembling housekeeper went into a flurry of apologies and pulled her handkerchief from her apron pocket.

"Master, I am so very sorry," she mumbled, wiping the tea from his sleeve.

"Not to worry." Hiram leaned down and picked up the ribbon, which had fallen from her pocket when she removed the hankie. "What is this?" Hiram held the ribbon before her. "Did you drop this?"

Eloise froze staring at the ribbon and then glanced to Daniel whose understanding eyes met hers. Eloise's fingers quivered pulling the ribbon from Hiram's hand.

"Sir, I will get the mop and the dustbin—no on second thought, I will wait till you have finished your conversation. Please excuse me." Eloise fled the scene, without thought of replacing the drinks.

Hiram stood looking suspiciously toward the door and then at Daniel, realizing that, once again, something questionable had transpired between his housekeeper and his best friend. Hiram passively looked over his damp sleeve and resumed his position across from Daniel, who avoided Hiram's inquisitive eyes. Hiram waited. Daniel finally explained while he carried the book back to the shelf.

"I doubt there e'er be a day that there 'tis not a wee bit of discomfort between Ellie and meself. The past can be an insidious intruder at times."

"Indeed, Miss Clayton paid me a visit when I was in Town. I understand that you delivered the letter from Mr. Zigmann."

Daniel nodded.

"Guillaume should have left well enough, alone. She arrived with high expectations and left sorely disappointed."

"Elizabeth is a lovely woman; she shan't be at a loss of good company for long."

"I shall never forget her expression—I am certain that it was very much like my own on the night that she ended our relationship."

Hiram and Daniel sat quietly for a minute before Daniel returned to the subject of the mysterious woman.

"Hiram, this woman, a lovely woman, in her looks and her manner—I met her in London."

"You rode all the way to Manchester with her?"

"We took the train," Daniel looked nervously away.

"What did your cousin Rupert think of your traveling companion?"

"His opinion? He was not there."

"Not there?"

"When we arrived that night, the cottage was boarded up."

"So... you stayed in Manchester?"

"Nay, we stayed at the cottage."

"With Rahzvon?"

"Nay, he did not show up till the next mornin'."

"Aye?" Hiram raised a brow.

"Now don't be thinkin' what yer thinkin'. I carried Birdy to her bed with the blasted beetles and she ended up in the master bedroom and me on the floor...in the parlor!"

"You need not explain, Daniel," Hiram readily insisted and in his discomfort scanned the room. "Birdy?"

"Aye, Birdy, 'She ne'er told me, her given name," Daniel mumbled.

"What did you say, Daniel?"

"I said, she ne'er told me!"

"Get a hold, man. Is there a problem with this woman?" Hiram asked with a teasing smile.

"She is a fine woman. In fact, Birdy was emphatic 'bout takin' the lad wit' us." Daniel calmed down and looked to the floor. "Ever find out what was troublin' him?"

"Aye, his father was a friend of mine. Gaelon was unjustly executed—the *demons*." Hiram rubbed his forehead with despair. "Rahzvon was then banished from his homeland."

"Ah, at the mercy o' a bad lot, poor lad. That explains his indifference; he ne'er spoke for half the journey. Birdy seemed to take to him."

"Did you leave her in Manchester?"

"Nay, Birdy is here, here in Lochmoor Glen. She is workin' at the Stewart home, up the road from the Wheaton farm."

Hiram straightened in his chair. "Why Daniel, I would like to make her acquaintance. The Stewarts are tenants of mine. I shall have to pay her a visit."

"She is a fine woman," Daniel repeated unconsciously, "but I would wait a bit. She is a private sort."

Daniel flashed back to her face. *A relative of Naomi, no doubt. You shall see, and then what?*

"Are you courting her, Daniel?"

"I asked if she'd consider correspondin' wit' me."

"Aye, did she agree?"

"She did." Daniel grinned.

Hiram left his seat to give Daniel a congratulatory pat on the back.

"Welcome to the world of *amour*, Daniel, where nothing is as it appears and every day tests your strength. Speaking of which, if you would not mind, I would like to ask you a question."

"Skip the formalities, Hiram, ya need not trouble yerself. Me sister is all yers. 'Tis a good thing, too. I am too old. Abby's been in me charge since she was two. There's not a better match for that ornery lassie. Ye will be needin' a strong constitution to be dealin' wit' her. She will argue with ya at ev'ry turn."

Hiram laughed, "Daniel, I do not know which will give me greater pleasure, having you for a brother-in-law or Abby for my wife," Hiram teased.

"Abby better not hear ya say that, or you shall be spendin' the first six months of yer marriage in one of yer many spare rooms."

"I would not doubt that for a minute, but she had better behave. I plan to take her to Deeside for a fortnight after the wedding," Hiram announced.

"Ah, Hiram, 'tis beautiful there— she will be forever indebted to ya."

"Abigail deserves the best, Daniel."

"Aye, Hiram, she does. And that is exactly what she will be gettin'.'"

Sophia and Abigail finished their dessert and retired to the parlor to wait for Hiram and Daniel to return. They sat anxiously next to the fireplace.

"Abigail, I do not understand your nervous state. Look at you, fidgeting. Do you not think Daniel will agree to your marriage? It is his dream come true, having his best friend marry his sister."

"I know Daniel will agree. Only, I am having difficulty believing that this wedding is really to take place."

"Why? Uncle Hiram loves you and you love him?"

"Yes, but your Uncle and I have had to overcome so many obstacles. I am not confident that one more shan't appear before the wedding."

"I do not believe my ears. Abigail O'Leardon, I am *astonished*. *You*, woman of the world, a woman who held her ground at every turn is *panicking*? This is not at all exemplary of your character. Do you not desire to be mistress of this house, aunt to the most loving niece you could ever encounter and wife of Britain's most admired and handsome man?"

"Yes."

"Then, the Abigail O'Leardon with whom I am acquainted shan't allow anything or anyone stop this wedding. Do you agree?"

Abigail smiled with conviction. "You are absolutely right, Sophia, we *will* have our wedding." She straightened in her chair, smoothed her skirt and sat back with a calm, collected expression.

"I so wish Rahzvon and I could marry," Sophia lamented.

"You will. He needs time to get his affairs in order. A man wants to be prepared to provide a good home for his family."

"Do you think you will have one, Abigail?"

"One?"

"A family. I know it is improper for one to ask, but I would like to know if, someday, I may have a cousin."

Abigail blushed, "Your uncle and I have not discussed that subject. I *have* seen him with the

Wheaton children; he seems to enjoy entertaining them."

"Uncle Hiram would be an excellent father; I am the perfect example of his parenting."

"Sophia!" Abigail warned when Hiram and Daniel appeared in the archway.

"Perfect example, eh?" Hiram cut in.

Sophia turned to his reply and shrugged. Abigail looked nervously toward the fireplace when her brother addressed Sophia.

"Sophia, would ye care to join me in a game o' cards in the study?"

Sophia flashed a smile at her uncle and rushed off to join Daniel. Hiram watched them leave and then sat down across from Abigail.

"Pleasant fire," he commented casually.

"Very pleasant," Abigail agreed. "It is a pleasant room, as well."

"Aye... although, I have been sorely tempted to move father," Hiram looked up to the portrait hanging above the mantle, "to the third floor."

"Is it not customary for the portrait of the Master of the house to be displayed in such a prominent position?"

"Aye, however, I have fought tradition for years. I think that I would prefer to cast my eyes on the likeness of the most beautiful woman in the world. I shall have the beauty of the mistress of this house adorning my parlor. Do you approve?" Hiram asked.

"I could answer that question with greater accuracy if I was certain as to whom you were making reference," she replied innocently.

Hiram stared at her for a few seconds then replied, "Delilah."

"Hiram McDonnally!" Abigail flew from her chair to attack him, for his insolence.

Hiram pulled her down to his lap and kissed her.

Abigail pulled back, "I do not want to hear that woman's name again!"

"You shan't until we attend her wedding in December, as a happily married couple."

"Hiram," Abigail melted into his embrace.

"What did you believe your brother and I were discussing?"

"With Daniel it could be the assassination of the editor of that French newspaper or the first performance of Pygmalion!"

"Aye, now, *off* with you lassie." He pushed her from his lap.

"I beg your pardon?"

"A carriage will be waiting for you in..." he pulled out his pocket watch, "a quarter hour."

"But, Hiram?"

"No questions. Make haste."

Hiram kissed her forehead and hustled her off to change her clothing. Hiram and Abigail disappeared behind the doors of their respective rooms to prepare for a second attempt to the beginning of their life together.

Avoiding Daniel, Eloise cleaned up the mishap in the study after he and Sophia finished their card game. Eloise returned to the kitchen and pulled the ribbon from her apron pocket, examining the tatted design.

"What do you have there?"

Startled, she looked up at her husband, Albert, then to the ribbon. "A piece of ribbon."

"A piece of ribbon?"

"I found it in a volume in the study."

"I think that you should return it. Someone may have marked a page and find it missing."

"They already have," Eloise mumbled.

"Eh, Ellie?"

"I shall return it tomorrow, Albert."

"Are you finished?" Albert asked.

"Yes, I am finished with my obligations." *Yes, Albert my obligation to Daniel is over.* Eloise took off her apron, hung it on the peg by the pantry and took Albert's hand to walk to the cottage behind the manor house. Eloise was genuinely relieved that her past relationship with Daniel O'Leardon was over. He had surrendered her aged ribbon from the sanctity of his wallet.

Hiram, donning all white, prepared to propose, parked the carriage in front of his home to wait for Abigail.

Perhaps she does not desire to reside here, after we are married. He looked over the grounds skeptically. *'Tis a bit dreary. I could have another home built—possibly atop Duncan Ridge.* He studied the façade of the home of his youth. *No, there is no need for Abby and I to continue living here.*

The mansion door opened and the doorway framed the illuminated figure of the future Mrs. Hiram McDonnally. Hiram jumped from the carriage after recovering from the initial shock of her exquisite appearance.

"Miss O'Leardon, you take my breath away!"

Abigail, lost in his equally awe-inspiring countenance, reached for his arm.

"Sir, there are not words in my vocabulary to convey my feelings at this moment."

Hiram raised a brow and walked with her to the carriage. Hiram looked to the sky. *Cloudy. Blasted, looks like rain.*

Once comfortably seated, Hiram set Hunter into a steady clip. Neither of the enamored couple spoke for several minutes. After they passed the Wheaton farm, Hiram inquired.

"Abby?"

"Yes, Hiram?"

"Do you have a preference as to where we reside after we are married?"

"I beg your pardon, sir? I do not recall ever consenting to be your wife. In fact, I have no memory of a proper marriage proposal." Abigail looked away, annoyed that her escort had forgone the traditional method of requesting her consent before discussing their future together.

Hiram snapped the reins and closed his eyes, momentarily, lamenting his stupidity in presenting the question *prior to* his "perfect" proposal plan.

Why do I make these foolish mistakes? His regrets dashed from his brain when Abigail let out a blood-curdling scream.

"Aghh!"

Hiram's eyelids flew open at the exact moment that the left side of the carriage dropped suddenly and the reins were pulled from his hands. Hiram was hurled from the carriage seat with Abigail sliding and rolling along with him into a heap in the ditch. The well-trained horse bolted, but stopped with the carriage a short distance down the road. Hiram lay face down in the muddy trench with the wind knocked out of him. Slowly he opened his eyes, trying desperately to lift his head.

"Ah, nay, not my back," he murmured in his dazed state. "Abby, where are you? Are you injured?" He tried to move his head again, side to side.

Abigail did not reply. He tried to look over his shoulder when he caught sight of a strawberry blonde ringlet on his arm.

"Abby?"

She did not respond.

"Abby!" he panicked, turning gently as her limp body slipped from his back to the ground beside him. Hiram ran his fingers across her cheek, desperately searching her face for a sign of life, when soft-spoken words slipped from her lips.

"A healing kiss would be appreciated," Abigail opened her eyes and smiled up at him.

"Abby," he said tenderly as his lips touched hers. "Are you injured?"

"No, I am well."

Hiram fell back with relief. They lay there quietly recovering, staring up at the clouds hovering overhead. The song of birds serenading in the treetops were accompanied by the refrain of a nearby brook bubbling over century-old pebbles.

"Listen, Abby, do you hear that?"

"Yes, Hiram, it is lovely."

Hiram reached for Abigail's hand and closed his gently around it.

"Hiram, I never imagined that loving someone could give you such a powerful sense of comfort and security," she said lying in the ditch.

"Aye, Abby."

The ominous clouds had crept above them and showered a sprinkling of fine rain. They remained, refreshed by the cool mist in the muck. Several minutes passed, and then Abigail sat up, pushing herself to balance on the bank. She looked hopelessly at her new dress, now torn and soiled beyond repair. Hiram stood up above her in his once white suit, filthy and drenched from the summer rain. Abigail did not move. They stared silently at one another.

My bonnie lassie. It is now or never, he thought.

Hiram dropped down on one knee, which sank deep into the mud. He reached out and carefully took her wet hand in his. Abigail was mesmerized by his unexpected position. She looked at him longingly, waiting for him to speak.

Hiram squeezed her hand tenderly and cleared his throat. Stripped of the confidence he had gained over the past weeks, he looked fearfully to her. Abigail's heart was singing with every word as he struggled.

"Abigail...Miss O'Leardon, would you...would you, *please,* do me the honor of becoming my wife, my beloved wife?"

Abigail smiled sweetly.

"Yes, Mr. McDonnally."

"You *would?*" Hiram asked cautiously.

"I should like nothing better."

Hiram pulled his future bride into his chest and ran his fingers through her fallen curls and sighed.

"I do not believe that I could survive yet another attempt to propose."

Abby threw her head back and laughed as he lifted her from the ground. He dug his boots into the soggy bank and carried her down the road to the carriage.

"Thank the Lord, Miss O'Leardon. It is done."

Abby looked over his shoulder.

"Wait, Hiram. Turn around."

Hiram turned.

"Look, it was a crack in the road."

"Aye, blasted, old roads."

"No, Hiram. I love that rut; I wish that I could take it home with us. It inspired the most romantic proposal. I shall never forget it."

Hiram turned and Abigail offered a kiss of consent without thought to the mud, the downpour or their overall unsightly appearance. Their display of affection may have continued indefinitely, had it not been interrupted by the familiar whoopla of Sophia and Rahzvon approaching on horseback. The young couple halted their horses and exchanged uncertain expressions with the unexpected scene.

Sophia observed Abigail's condition and immediately asked, "Abigail, have you broken your leg or something?"

Abby smiled and tightened her arms around her fiancés neck.

"No, I am perfectly fine. We fell in the ditch," she said with sheer content.

Sophia raised her brows, looked to Rahzvon, and grinned.

"Your new dress, Abigail, it is a mess," Sophia noted with regret.

"Yes, I may never change; I may wear it forever. I will remember this day for the rest of my life."

"Sophia, Rahzvon, your timing is impeccable," Hiram greeted them with a broad smile. "May you be the first to congratulate us!"

Sophia pursed her lips, and then asked, "Congratulate you?"

"Yes, may I present to you, the future Mrs. Hiram McDonnally? She has accepted my proposal." He heaved Abigail up on to the seat of the carriage as the rain stopped.

"Ah, yes, a fine choice, indeed," Rahzvon teased.

"Now see here, *Ahab*," Abigail shook her finger at Rahzvon. "Rumor has it, that I shan't be the only visitor to arrive at the McDonnally Manor in less than pristine attire."

Rahzvon responded confidently, "I cannot contradict you, Miss O'Leardon. It was not too many weeks past that Miss Sophia returned to McDonnally Manor in a rather disheveled state."

"Rahzvon!" Sophia objected.

"Yes," he continued, "wearing Zigmann's trousers, my ganzer and..." he reached over and gently patted her face, "a fresh layer of dust. If I recall, it was after a rather exciting journey to Grimwald."

"We like our women looking as natural as possible. Do you not agree, Rahzvon?" Hiram chimed in.

"Most definitely."

Hiram and Rahzvon laughed.

Sophia rolled her eyes, "We should be going; I promised Naomi that I would bathe Heidi. We will see you later. Congratulations Uncle, Abigail."

"At least one member of the clan will be clean!" Hiram called out.

Hiram pulled a woolen blanket from under the seat of the carriage and wrapped it around Abigail.

"Does this remind you of anything, Hiram?"

"If you are referring to the day that you were lost on the moors, I would rather not discuss it."

"I have caused you a lot of grief, Hiram." She brushed his wet curls back from his forehead. "But

I can promise you that life will never be boring with me as your wife, Hiram."

"Of that, you do not have to convince me, Abby. I have had more excitement over the last few months with you, than I have had in all the years of my life." He gave her a kiss on the cheek and took the reins.

Chapter 111

"Experience"

"And shall they sketch your picture
With comic truth the while,
Be sad and look severely on–
The teacher mustn't smile."

—H. Clarence Gibbs

It was a balmy mid-morning of the last day of May. Hiram accepted the responsibility of substituting for his uncle to carry out what appeared to be a relatively simple task. Edward, a mere eight years older than Hiram, was scheduled to make the semi-annual visit to review the school's supply and repair list with Lochmoor Glen's only school teacher, Miss Nettlepin. The McDonnally clan had generously committed to the building and maintenance of the Hillside School and funding for the academic materials.

Edward, still recovering from an accidental fall, failed to arm his nephew with any information about the socially illusive educator. This negligence on Edward's part was highly suspect. However, the innocent nephew agreed, without question, to meeting with the woman for the first time that morning.

Hiram tied his horse to a tree north of the cottage and knocked on the door. A spindly woman in her late forties appeared wearing her hair in a tight bun, spectacles and fitted tweed jacket and skirt. She peered over the rims of her glasses and greeted the expected visitor.

"Do come in, Mr. McDonnally."

"Thank you, Miss Nettlepane."

"*Pin*, Nettlepin," she corrected. "Hiram, you may call me Iris, like the flower."

"Excuse me, but have we met?"

"Not formally, but I have watched you—I mean to say, *observed* your presence in the village," she explained.

Hiram quirked a brow.

"Will you take tea with me, sir?"

"That really is not necessary, Miss...Iris."

"Oh, but it is. I spent all morning preparing sweets for you," she said sternly.

"Of course, then, I would be delighted," he said with as much sincerity as he could muster up.

"Very well, if you will excuse me and have a seat on the divan, I will return shortly," she announced sharply.

Hiram sat down and glanced around the room. Framed portraits covered the walls and tables.

Her whole clan? Brothers, uncles, cousins, no women, only men, he thought with curiosity. He picked up a small gilded frame placed on the table in front of him.

"Great Scott, it is *Edward,*" he whispered. He studied it carefully. It was an excellent rendition in pen and ink. *I must commend her on her artistry,* he thought as he replaced it to the table. He looked to the right. There on the table next to him was another frame, larger than the one displaying Edward's likeness. Hiram held it up to the light from the window. *Jon Wiggins? The butcher?* He sat it down. There was another on the wall. "Mr. Kilvert, the postman?" *Does she have every confounded male member of the village in here?*

Although it initially struck him as peculiar, he soon rationalized that her extraordinary talent excused the fact that she displayed her miniature masterpieces in the privacy of her parlor.

Excuses for her strange behavior, however, ended abruptly when the once well-groomed Miss Nettlepin appeared in the doorway with a silver tray stacked with sweets enough to satisfy ten men. The abundant tray was not the object of his scrutiny. The hostess had not only shed her spectacles; her tweed jacket, had been replaced with a brightly colored blouse and several long strands of green beads. This was a bit shocking, but not half as disturbing as the newly applied bright lip rouge unevenly tracing her lips and the mousy brown, gray-streaked hair drooping down over her shoulders. To make matters worse, the repulsive scent of cheap scented water, now dominating the air, accompanied this unpleasant image. Hiram involuntarily rose to his feet at the shock of her appearance. To cover for his unexpected response, he immediately offered to take the tray.

Miss Nettlepin smiled sheepishly, "I can see that you are genuinely surprised; they usually are. I thought that being better acquainted, I shan't hide my true identity," she said coyly.

I wish you had.

Hiram sat the tray down on the table trying to focus on anything, but her new face.

She sat down on the divan next to him, poured a cup of tea, and offered it to him. He lifted the cup from her hand.

"Iris, perhaps we should discuss the matters at hand. I understand that you maintain a well-disciplined classroom."

"Such large, masculine hands; a large beer stein would seem more appropriate than a delicate china cup," she said softly and reached across and caressed his hand.

Hiram became fixated on her misshapen mouth and replied, "I do not partake in drinking."

"How positively refreshing—a clear-minded gentleman."

Clear-minded? Hardly, why I cannot even think of way to escape, graciously.

"I like that—nothing to *disturb* this lovely brain," she tapped his temple with her index finger and grinned.

Hiram cringed at her touch.

You *are disturbing my brain, woman. I have to get out of here,* he began to panic. He stared at Edward's face before him with deepening anger. *You will pay for sending me into this lair.*

At this point, Hiram's flight response was fully engaged and the only blockade between him and the door was his proper upbringing as a gentleman. He sipped his tea trying to calm his nerves. When he believed the situation could not get any worse, she left her place beside him and walked behind the divan. Like a cat with a mouse, she began toying with his hair. He immediately flinched nearly spilling his drink.

"Excuse me, what are you doing?" he asked nervously.

"Do not mind me, I find if I experience them, it facilitates my ability to reproduce the locks on paper," she explained calmly.

Experience them?

Her hands moved to his shoulders and patted them lightly. She then resumed her position next to him.

"I am an *artist,*" she said proudly.

"Aye, your work... it is quite...quite realistic."

"Hiram, could you please prepare a cup for me?"

"Now, might we discuss the school's needs, Miss Nettlepin?"

"*Iris.* Two sugars, please, Hiram."

He felt his efforts were in vain and feared he was becoming a puppet to her every whim. He tried to steady his large fingers and grasped the small tongs to place two lumps in her cup. He picked up the pot and tilting the lid, began to pour. Nothing came out. He vented the lid further. Nothing. He replaced the teapot to the table. It was empty. He realized, once again, that nothing about this visit was normal or predictable.

"Oh, dear, is it empty?" she asked with surprise.

"Aye," Hiram mumbled with suspicion.

"I shall have to prepare more. Excuse me, Hiram."

Hiram sat in a daze. He felt as though he had been there for at least a week. Then, he realized his opportunity had arrived.

Should I run like the wind or should I announce that I am leaving?

He got up from the couch and moved swiftly to the door. He reached for the door handle.

What will I tell Edward about the report? Hiram glanced at the framed image of Edward smiling smugly up at him. *I know what I will tell him— I will give him a piece of my mind!*

"Hiram, oh, Hiram!"

Now, what does she have up her sleeve? I am not staying to find out. I am leaving.

"Help me, Hiram! Please, Hiram!" she called from the kitchen.

Although his instincts demanded that he not wait a moment longer to escape, he knew that it would be a scandal if he abandoned her in her hour of need. He looked around helplessly like a scared rabbit. He swallowed hard and stepped into the kitchen. She was not there.

"In here!" she called from the pantry.

Hiram glared at the curtains on the doorway.

It is a trap! I can feel it with every bone in my body.

"Hurry, Hiram I cannot hang on much longer!"

Hiram closed his eyes for a moment, and then entered through the curtains. The gypsy-like form balanced on one foot on the third shelf, hung precariously by the two supporting shelf boards.

"Miss Nettlepin, what are you doing *up there*?" he stared in astonishment.

"The stool broke, when I was reaching for the tea," she claimed. Hiram glanced at the two-legged stool lying on the floor. Strangely enough, he could not locate the third leg; it was not in the pantry.

"Please help me down," she begged.

Dare he walk away? The decision to help her was a difficult one. Making physical contact with *this* woman was, without question, less than desirable.

"Hiram, please!" she pleaded.

He acted in the name of pure chivalry, no matter how foolish it may have been. He took a breath of courage and reached up to her. Her satin sleeves slithered around him. One rested on his shoulder; the other strategically across his chest. She pressed her face next to his. The repugnant cologne was nauseating his stomach to near retaliation. He started to stand her to the floor when she attached herself like a leach.

"On to the divan, I may have strained something!" she demanded.

Hiram was dropping her to the couch after six quick strides. He then opened his jacket and fumbled with his pocket watch.

"Mr. McDonnally, you would not consider leaving, would you?" she reprimanded as she sat up. "We have yet to discuss the school. I simply cannot allow it. Sit *down!*"

"My apologies, Miss Nettlepin," he said moving quickly towards the door. "You understand, it has been lovely, but I have another engagement with my uncle—a *pressing* engagement. I will let myself out."

"When shall we reschedule?" she called out.

"*Edward* will handle the arrangements. Good day, Miss Nettlepane."

"Pin, Nettlepin!"

Hiram fled from the cottage and untied Hunter. He mounted and rode full speed in the direction of Brachney Hall.

The unabashed teacher returned to her kitchen, snatched up her glasses and returned to the chair at her writing table. She withdrew a piece of paper from the drawer and dipped her pen.

"*Hiram McDonnally.* This could be my final contribution to my collection. Once Hiram and I are residing at the manor, I highly doubt that he will approve of my sketching *other* men."

Miss Nettlepin began humming while she created a remarkably accurate rendering of her last guest.

Hiram's relentless pounding nearly removed the doors from the hinges at Brachney Hall. Naomi carefully opened the door.

"Where is he?" the infuriated nephew demanded.

Naomi withered at his booming echo in the hall.

"Edward?" she asked fearfully.

"Aye!" Hiram plowed past her to the parlor. She followed in horror, having witnessed Hiram's ill temper at McDonnally Manor where he had left the parlor in a state of rubble.

"If you were not in that chair, I *would*—" Hiram bellowed.

"Now, nephew," Edward grasped the wheels of his chair, "remember, I am a helpless invalid!"

"Helpless, indeed! We shall see how helpless you are!"

"No!" Naomi took a stance between them.

Edward intervened, "Naomi, calm down. All shall be fine. Take Heidi for a walk; this is a private matter."

"Aye, you do not want to witness what I am about to do to this *traitor*," Hiram warned.

Naomi looked uncomfortably at Hiram's threatening expression and left reluctantly, praying that the strength of Edward and Hiram's kinship would prevail. She searched the rooms, summoning her little dachshund, her voice barely audible above the name-calling in the parlor. *What has Edward done, this time?* She returned to the hall, against her better judgment.

"Hiram, you certainly cannot hold me responsible for Miss Nettlepin's attraction to wealthy, good-looking men." Edward reasoned.

"Attraction? The woman is positively ravenous!"

Hiram began pacing with an attempt to gain control of his temper. "And you are mistaken if you believe that she targets only the wealthy! Jon Wiggins was one of her victims. The *butcher*, mind you."

"Ah, the miniatures," Edward remembered.

"Edward, are you aware that your likeness is displayed as one of her *trophies*?"

"Really? I say, our teacher is quite the little artist. Is it a *good* likeness?"

Hiram stopped pacing and took a breath. "You find this all very amusing, do you not? All at *my* expense."

"Hiram, old man, where is your sense of humor? Miss Nettlepin is harmless."

"Sense of humor! Harmless? Then what possessed you to engage me as your replacement for this *harmless* mission? Answer that!"

"Nephew, I appeal to your sense of fair play. Do I appear to be in any condition to defend myself against Miss Nettlepin's hospitality? By the appearance of your cheek, I would wager that even the *Grand* Master of McDonnally Manor had apparent difficulty in dealing with the little lady," Edward chuckled.

"What are you implying?" Hiram demanded.

"She left her mark. You had better do something about it, old boy, before Abigail spots it. Look in the hall mirror," Edward snickered.

Hiram scowled and walked to the hall.

"Blast her!" He rubbed the lip rouge from his cheek and return to confront his offender.

"You shall pay, *dear* uncle."

"Speaking of payment, dare I ask how the committee of one faired in discussing the condition of the school?" Edward teased.

Hiram narrowed his eyes and shook his head with contempt.

"If you were not a McDonnally, Edward, you would not be enjoying the safety of that wheeled chair." Hiram began to pace again. "This experience makes one consider growing back one's beard."

"Hiram, they flock to you like moths to a flame, with or without the beard. Besides, in two or three decades, you may delight in the attention of the Miss Nettlepins of this world."

"Moths *flock*? Never, never again, do you hear me?" He shook his finger at Edward, sitting defiantly with his arms folded. "Understand this, Edward McDonnally; I shan't meet with any woman with whom I have *not* met previously."

"Then you shan't have any objection to delivering the monthly allotment to Miss Nettlepin," Edward taunted.

If looks could kill, Edward would have passed into the next life many times that afternoon.

"Very, well, I apologize, but I am curious, old man... did our proper schoolmarm require assistance in the *pantry*, during your visit? More sugar, perhaps?" Edward asked suppressing a smile.

"More *tea*," Hiram nodded.

The two men stared at one another, reading each other's thoughts of their visits with the creative teacher. It started small, but quickly developed into a room quaking with hysteria as they broke into uncontrolled laughter.

"Your...your *hair*—did she?" Edward struggled, wiping the tears from his eyes, and holding his aching ribs.

"Ex...experience it?" Hiram howled, now bent over in stitches. "Can you, can you imagine W... Wiggins?" Hiram forced between breaths.

Now, the red-faced Edward could barely breathe, let alone speak.

Hiram fell into the couch holding his side, "Wonder...wonder what she said when she...she ran her fingers through his, his to...to..." Hiram doubled over.

"Toupee!" Edward burst out.

Naomi stood in the archway, absorbed in the display of the two wealthiest men in Scotland coming apart at the seams in their intoxicating amusement. Grinning, she folded her arms and shook her head.

I would not have accepted a million dollars to miss this opportunity.

Chapter IV

"Cast Off"

"Many are the afflictions
Of the righteous;
But the Lord delivereth
him out of them all."

Brachney Hall, already bubbling with excitement of the newest residents, Patience and the tiny "Dest", was a scene of anticipation and celebration. Dr. Lambert was scheduled to remove the cumbersome casts from Edward's limbs in the next few hours. Naomi arrived with Heidi, at half past eight.

"Edward!" Naomi called.

"I am in here, love," Edward replied from the library.

Naomi found him at the table with a dozen opened books lying before him. He was thumbing through one when Naomi entered the room.

"What are you reading, love?" she asked.

"No questions. Come here and give me my morning kiss."

Naomi obliged and then rushed to the little basket beneath the window. She knelt down with Heidi by her side and stroked Patience and her kitten.

"Patience appears to be feeling better."

"I agree. A good rest in a clean warm basket and your love is all that she needed, Naomi."

"Is it not odd that Patience stole Heidi and carried her to McDonnally Manor and now, Heidi returned the favor and carried Dest home to Brachney Hall."

"Naomi you have to know that Dest is not Patience's kitten."

"I know, Patience is old and she probably found him."

"Stole, more than likely. She probably snatched it from a neighbor's barn."

"It does not matter to me, where he is from. I intend to love him and take care of him."

"Yes, you shall, but for the present time you need to leave them to their own amusement and entertain your poor fiancé."

"My poor fiancé is about to relinquish his sympathy card and begin taking care of *me*."

Naomi set the table and unloaded the breakfast basket. "We should have enough time to finish our meal before the doctor arrives." Naomi spread the butter on a piece of brown bread.

"I hope we can find a cook as talented as Eloise, Naomi."

"You can always give her lessons, Master of *Broccoli Hall*," Naomi teased when the doorknocker sounded. "Right on time."

A servant answered the door and announced the arrival of a tall, young woman, instead of the doctor. Naomi met them in the hall. "Hello, may I help you?"

"Good morning. I am looking for Mr. Guillaume Zigmann?"

Edward wheeled up behind Naomi with a Cheshire grin. "Mr. Guillaume Zigmann?"

"Yes, Mr. McDonnally said that he was here."

"He is here. However, he is out at the tool shed. Should I have him summoned?" Edward asked.

"No, that is not necessary. I can speak with him there... with your permission."

"Take the flagstone path out back, down to the pond. The shed is off to the left. You cannot miss it," Edward explained.

"Thank you, I shall be going now." She nodded and started to leave.

Naomi looked at the visitor with concern and extended her hand, "May I introduce myself? I am Naomi McDonnally."

"Oh, are you the wife of the gentleman at McDonnally Manor?"

"No, no I am his—this is my husband, Edward McDonnally."

"My pleasure, I am Trina Dunmore."

Naomi stood stunned. *Guillaume's past fiancé?* She made a quick recovery greeting. "Hello, Trina."

"I hope to meet with you again, very soon," Trina remarked as she left. She went out to the awaiting carriage to notify the driver.

Naomi turned slowly toward Edward.

Edward mumbled, "What comes around goes around... to the back of the house and out to the shed."

"Allison is going to be furious," Naomi shook her head.

"And Guillaume is a cooked goose," Edward added solemnly.

As Naomi closed the door, the doctor's carriage pulled in behind Trina's.

"The doctor is here, Edward." Naomi's concern with Trina disappeared as she cheerfully invited the physician into the mansion. "Welcome, Dr. Lambert."

"We have been counting the minutes for this day," Edward reported.

"'Tis the best part o' me job, other than bringin' the bairn' into the world."

"Get the saw and get on with it, Doctor." Edward commanded. "Well, rather, off with it!"

"First, a wee warnin'. These limbs shall appear smaller than yer other arm and leg, because they are. But, 'tis only temporary, as you begin to exercise them again. Ye need to build up the muscle tissue."

Naomi spoke up. "I shall see that he gets in several walks a day and as for the arm, I have a number of crates, I need brought down from the third floor. I was going to ask a servant to assist me, but Edward shall do quite nicely," she teased. The three moved to the kitchen.

With precision cutting, Dr. Lambert gently removed the cast from Edward's arm.

"Ye may want to fetch a pail o' warm water and soap. It shan't be pleasant."

Naomi collected towels and all the necessities to clean Edward's arm. Slowly, Edward's mended arm came into view as the doctor laid the two halves of the cast on the table and unwound the remaining bandages. Edward made a slight grimace at the sight of his shrunken arm, but Naomi ignored the stench and began cleaning.

"I'll give it a thorough check when yer finished Mrs. McDonnally." The doctor began working on Edward's leg cast.

Noting Edward's disappointment in the condition of his arm, Naomi said cheerily, "Edward McDonnally, I can only imagine how marvelous it feels to have the weight removed."

"Sorry you had to witness this, Naomi," Edward said pitifully.

"It is my duty as a wife. I do not mind in the least." She continued gently scrubbing away the dead skin. "There, is that not much better? Ready for examination, doctor," she announced while patting Edward's arm with the towel.

"Verra good, ye wouldna be interested in becomin' me assistant?" the doctor joked.

"From the looks of this arm, I think I shall be needed here. Besides, we have a new baby to attend to."

The doctor looked at them with astonishment.

Edward broke in, "A kitten, doctor."

"Aye, I thought me ol' memory was failin' me more than usual," he added while placing the stethoscope on Edward's chest.

"Yer lookin' good, lad."

Naomi smiled at the report. Edward nodded.

"Now, this shall be a wee more difficult. Mrs. McDonnally, please help steady the leg and support it. Edward, remain as still as ye can."

The doctor began sawing at the cast into several sections, then slicing it down the side. It was a slow process, but ended with excellent results.

"Edward, all ye shall be needin' is exercise. Take it easy at first. Spend a great deal of time restin' in the next few days."

"You hear that Naomi? It appears that you shall have to be attending to me for quite some time, yet. I shan't over exert myself."

Naomi agreed, "Definitely not, Edward. You may assist the servants. You can perform simple tasks, such as drying dishes and folding linens to strengthen your arm."

"Hold on! Doctor, do you not think that I should restrict my schedule to reading and perhaps working with my stamp collection?"

Dr. Lambert grinned, "Yer, at her, mercy, lad. Ye wouldna want to anger her before the weddin'." He laid the cast on the floor and removed the last bandage strip. Naomi washed and dried his leg preparing for the final check.

"I think ye shall be back to yerself wit'out any difficulty. Aye, this leg has healed verra well," the doctor explained, gently lifting and moving Edward's leg into numerous positions.

Naomi burst out laughing. Edward immediately took offense, "This puny leg shall soon be a perfect match for the other! I shall see to it!"

Naomi, soon gained control and explained, "No love, I was not laughing at your leg. Look," she pointed to the cast beside the table.

The doctor and Edward joined in her amusement in seeing the little dachshund comfortably stretched out in the confines of one of the cast pieces.

"Dr. Lambert, perhaps, you should abandon your practice and sell dachshund beds," Edward laughed. "It could be a lucrative business."

"I shall have to start savin' 'em and have Mrs. Lambert paint wee flowers on 'em. We shall be standin' ye up, now. Put yer arms around me and then Naomi."

Edward placed his weight on his good leg and stood in front of the chair.

"Feels light as a feather," Edward commented as he shifted to the mended leg.

"Ah, this is better," he looked down on Naomi. "At last, I feel like the man of the house again." Edward puffed out his chest.

"You may be towering over me, but as your nurse, I am still in charge," Naomi reminded.

Naomi could not bring herself to dispose of Heidi's newly acquired sleeping quarters. She removed the pup, cleaned it, lined it with a towel and placed it by the basket occupied by the two cats. To Naomi's dismay, Heidi immediately gave the new bed a thorough sniffing, ignored it, and removed the towel to arrange it in a heap on the floor. The little dog circled three times and curled up on it, and closed her eyes.

"There goes the dog bed business," Dr. Lambert noted. After a few minutes of therapeutic instruction, he began packing up his tools.

At the shed, Guillaume fought to remove a rusted nail from a board. "You are coming out, *now!*" He gave another tug with the hammer, looked up and took a double take out the hazy pane. He squinted to focus on the familiar woman moving toward him down the flagstone path. *No, no, not, not Trina?* he cringed. When she appeared in the doorway, Guillaume stepped back in horror and dropped the hammer. He let out a wail of pain when it landed precisely on his toe.

"Aghh!

After a series of single-footed hops, Guillaume sat down on the tool chest, pulled off his shoe and rubbed his toe.

"Trina...uh...what are you...*Ow*...doing here?"

"You did not answer my letters, Guillaume. I felt that seeing me, in person—"

"Trina, you have to leave, *now!*"

"Very well, I shall see you later." She turned to leave.

"No, Trina, you have to leave Lochmoor Glen. You have to leave Scotland."

"I am not going anywhere, Mr. Zigmann. I am here to stay," she said confidently and left the shed.

Guillaume snarled behind her back and hopped up to the house in time to catch Dr. Lambert.

"What has happened to ya, Guillaume?" the doctor asked.

Only a hurt toe, but after I speak with Allison, you can prepare a hospital bed for me."

Chapter V

"For Hire"

"Nor how the cinders to the sky
Went whirling from the structure dry;
Nor how afar, at midnight's noon,
As giant snow-flakes they were strewn."

—H. Clarence Gibbs

Edward opened the letter from the London store clerk to reread the contents, thinking, *No, I probably should have not intercepted Naomi's letter...but finding her mother shall make up for the quilt and I* shall *have my perfect gift.*

> *Mrs. McDonnally,*
>   *The young man of whom you inquired, when you were visiting, returned to the shop this afternoon for some spools of cotton. I nearly forgot to ask him about his mother. He said that her name is "Beatrice."*

"Where's that address for Mr. Jorgensen? I need to get him on this immediately. I can see Naomi's face, *now.*"

Edward smiled and leaned back in the chair. However, in realizing that Naomi's mother had made a new life without Naomi, Edward reconsidered. He began slowly pacing back and forth across the room, reviewing any possible negative motives that Naomi may have for tracking down the mother who she had not seen since she was twelve years old. His indecision ended, being content to believe that Naomi did not have a vengeful bone in her body.

A knock at the door woke him from his thoughts. A servant greeted the visitor, directing her to the parlor.

"Mrs. Zigmann, *come in.* I have a proposition for you."

"Mr. McDonnally!" Eloise teased.

"Eloise, might you consider working for a new, more distinguished and unquestionably more handsome employer than my nephew, Hiram?"

"More handsome, than the Master?"

"Considerably."

"I cannot imagine. Who might this be, sir?" Eloise asked innocently.

Edward smiled broadly and with a proud air, displayed his profile.

Eloise giggled, "Mr. McDonnally, you are an incorrigible character. How does it feel to be on two legs again?"

"Empowering, but not enough to lure you away from my impressive nephew. Perhaps you can assist me in finding a cook. The woman I was to hire from Ireland, is now with child. The lassie in London wired that she was marrying and remaining there, and Mr. Kilvert's cousin...well, her husband is opposed to her working here—probably because I am so charming and irresistible."

"More than likely." Eloise grinned.

"Do you know of anyone?"

"I shall ask around the village. Maryanne Wheaton mentioned that the Stewarts recently hired a woman to do light housekeeping. Maybe they could spare her. Their cottage is quite small, she need only work for them a few hours a week."

"Grand! I would prefer to get this matter settled before the wedding. Thanks to Naomi's interviewing effort, the cleaning staff is adequate and Angus has trained the grounds men. A cook is our last position to fill."

"I have some errands to run. After Albert and I visit with the Dugans, we can make a stop at the Stewarts." She handed Edward a small covered basket. "It nearly slipped my mind—the raspberry tarts to celebrate your recovery."

"You are a gem, Eloise. Thank you. I certainly hope that my nephew does not take you for granted. And if he ever does, a new position awaits you here." Edward took a bite of the tart.

"I shan't forget. I must go now. Good day, Mr. McDonnally."

"Scrumptious, thank you!" Edward waved, taking another bite of the delectable treat.

Beatrice sat down on the porch swing at the Stewart home. She swung gently, admiring the waving wildflowers in the yard and the birds flitting playfully on the fence. Suddenly, a stream of smoke in the distance caught her eye when she looked up to see an arriving wagon.

"Good morning! We are the Zigmanns."

"Hello, I am ...Birdy. Excuse me, I have not lived here...for long. Do you see that smoke over there?" she pointed across the moors.

Albert and Eloise looked in that direction.

"Dear me, Albert, I think it is coming from the schoolhouse," Eloise gasped.

"We had better check into it. Good day, mum." Albert snapped the reins and Hunter trotted off.

"I shall talk to you later!" Eloise called out. Beatrice waved in return.

"A fire? Where?" Mrs. Stewart asked joining Beatrice on the porch.

"There." Beatrice pointed, "The Zigmanns say that they believe it may be the schoolhouse."

"Aye, ye shan't be o' use here. Hurry and fetch the pails from the well and take the wagon."

"Yes, Mrs. Stewart."

Beatrice ran to the well, unhooked the bucket and grabbed the one sitting on the back step. She tossed them into the back of the wagon and climbed aboard. Picking up the reins, she stopped, in a pensive stare.

What am I doing? What if Naomi is there? She tightened her grip on the reins and reconsidered. *No, why would a fine lady of society, assist in a fire brigade?*

"Gid up." Beatrice drove off keeping a close eye on the Zigmann wagon to direct her.

The Zigmanns arrived at the site of the schoolhouse to find several concerned families relaying bucket after bucket to the unrelenting blaze. Beatrice parked behind the Zigmann wagon and looked in dismay at the futile attempt. Most of the building was reduced to ashes while the remainder belched smoke into the once clear blue sky. The families abandoned all effort and stood back in horror at the sight. Their first school had been a simple one-room layout. The new larger facility saw the children through a mere three sessions before this fateful day.

Miss Nettlepin, stood stunned next to the *Hillside School* sign. Beatrice examined the distraught faces; Naomi's was not among them.

Eloise turned to Beatrice, "The school, an awful shame. Everyone here has school-age children, save Albert and me."

"Does anyone know how it started?"

"No, that shall come later. A few dozen children are without a school." Eloise shook her head. "Birdy, earlier, I was on my way to ask Mrs. Stewart if she could spare you to take an additional cooking position."

"Cooking position?"

"You can cook, can you not?"

"Yes."

"Another family is looking for someone to hire. Would you be willing, if Mrs. Stewart agrees?"

Beatrice looked away uneasily.

"Brachney Hall is not far, it is between the Stewart cottage and the village. Speak to Mrs. Stewart about it. It would be an excellent opportunity. You could not find better employers. I shall tell the McDonnallys that you are considering the position," Eloise said while Albert helped her to her seat.

Beatrice nodded to the Zigmanns and carried the two buckets back to the wagon. *The McDonnallys—my dear Naomi and her husband, Edward. Mrs. Wheaton mentioned that they were looking for someone for hire.* She looked toward the village. *How am I to avoid this?*

As the Zigmanns pulled away, Eloise inquired, "Albert, does she not favor, Mrs. McDonnally?"

"Very much so, Ellie." Eloise looked back suspiciously at the Stewart's housekeeper.

Beatrice's interest returned to the sullen families, exhausted and despondent. One by one, they drove off to their homes. Miss Nettlepin was the last to leave. She sat on a little bench under a tree in the schoolyard. Gentle winds swirled the ashes about her while her gaze was lost in the last few embers smoldering in the dirt. Beatrice walked over to her and placed a comforting hand on her shoulder.

"I am very sorry. I, too, know the pain of losing something that is very important." Beatrice sat down next to the silent woman.

"My apologies, I am Hillside's teacher, Miss Nettlepin." She closed her eyes and nodded briefly.

"I am Birdy, Mr. and Mrs. Stewart's new housekeeper."

"*Birdy?* What kind of name is *that?*" the teacher asked with certain negativity.

Beatrice was taken aback. Fortunately, Miss Nettlepin offered no time for an explanation.

"The students never liked me, but I did find the school adequate."

"There *is* time to rebuild before autumn," Beatrice encouraged.

"No funding available," Miss Nettlepin said sharply. "The only clan in the area that could afford to rebuild has already provided more than their share. The McDonnallys donated this property and all the materials to build this one. The families around here are too proud to ask for additional charity."

"The McDonnallys?"

"Yes, Edward and his nephew Hiram. Village gossip says that everyone expected Naomi to marry the nephew," the teacher lowered her voice, "but she ended up with Edward, the uncle. No doubt he is a fine gentleman, a bit liberal-minded for my taste."

"And the nephew?"

"You *obviously* have never seen the man." Miss Nettlepin looked over her spectacles.

"No, I have not. I only recent—"

"Yes, now there is a *man*." The teacher fell into a dazed state. "Tall, black curly hair, eyes that could—yes, Hiram McDonnally sat in my parlor, only recently and I believe he enjoyed every minute. So charming," she said dreamily. "Never mind, no explanation shall be necessary when you meet him."

Beatrice thought curiously, *Either the nephew is only remarkable in her eyes or she could only pray to be a source of his interest, if he truly is uncommonly handsome.*

"And why did she choose the uncle," Beatrice asked cautiously.

"How she let Hiram slip away, no one in Scotland can understand. Had I lived here then, I would be with Hiram, today. They were childhood sweethearts, Naomi and Hiram. Now, that Irish woman has latched on to him—not one of us is happy about it," she said spitefully. "Choose the uncle? I have only seen Naomi once. Mrs. Dugan said it had something to do with the scar on her face. No one knows how it happened."

Beatrice's hand went to her mouth in shock.

The teacher continued. "They are renewing their vows in a few days at the church, you know."

"A wedding?"

The teacher ignored her inquiry, "Our building, our primers, all gone. I would return to London, but I am not certain that Hiram would permit it. He said that he admires my abilities to maintain a well-disciplined classroom. Those were, in fact, his exact words. However, I understand that he does have a flat in Town."

"You think quite highly of Mr. McDonnally."

"I do, however, I must say that I am disturbed by his tolerance of the O'Leardon girl. She is *much* too young for him. He needs a more mature woman to care for him. One who understands his volatile temperament—not one who exasperates it," she said pointedly. "No, I shan't leave, he *shall* come to his senses. In the meantime I have a slew of lessons swimming in this brain," she pointed to her head. "Yes, the children shall continue their education without primers, once I procure a proper place to meet with them. After the wedding, the church shall be a viable alternative. I must go now and nap. We younger women need our rest to preserve our beauty."

Beatrice withheld any comment or display of her amusement with the unusual teacher.

"I am sorry we had to meet under such dire circumstances, Miss Nettlepin."

"Indeed, it is tragic, but, every cloud, as they say—this fire may be the only avenue to our reunion."

"Our reunion?"

"Not ours. Hiram's and mine," she clarified. "Good day." She walked away proudly with her nose to the sky.

"Good day, Miss Nettlepin." Beatrice returned to the wagon and drove from the catastrophic scene.

The next day, Edward left Brachney Hall with plans of his own to discuss sharing the Stewart housekeeper. When he arrived, Mrs. Stewart met him on the front steps.

"Mr. McDonnally."

"Good morning, Mrs. Stewart."

"C'mon in. Did ye hear 'bout the fire at the schoolhouse?"

"Yes, Albert Zigmann informed me. A tragedy for the village families."

"I shall get tea."

"Thank you, Mrs. Stewart."

Mrs. Stewart returned from the kitchen. "Sir, what brings ye here?" she asked skeptically.

"I would like to discuss a matter of business with you and your husband. My wife and I are seeking to hire a cook. We need someone to fill the position after the wedding. Mrs. Zigmann mentioned that you could possibly spare your chorewoman. She would still be available to perform her housekeeping duties for you. However, rest assured that I have no desire to inconvenience you by having her in my employ."

"I wouldna agree to any arrangement that would be inconveniencin' me, Mr. McDonnally, despite yer nephew ownin' this place."

"Yes, Madame, I mean, no, Madame."

"Miss Birdy is a hard worker. She is verra thorough and efficient. She *is* a fair cook. She can return to clean for a few hours on Wednesdays and Saturdays. We canna afford to feed her, as it is."

"Is she here? I would like to be introduced." Edward looked around the room.

"Nay, she is runnin' an errand to the Wheaton's. She shall be reportin' to Brachney Hall on the first Monday after yer weddin'."

"Thank you, Mrs. Stewart. I know Mrs. McDonnally shall appreciate your generosity as much as I."

"A business arrangement is all it is."

"Yes...thank you for the tea, Mrs. Stewart."

"Ye havna tasted it."

Edward smiled and quickly took a sip.

"Again, thank you and now I must be going. I hope to see you and Mr. Stewart at the wedding."

"Depends on me husband's health."

"Please tell him I send my regards and tell Miss..."

"Birdy."

"Please, tell Miss Birdy that she is welcome to attend our wedding. Good day, Mrs. Stewart and thank you."

Edward left feeling that it was not a minute too soon. Mrs. Stewart watched him leave and mumbled, "McDonnallys, *humph*, them an' their high an' mighty attitudes."

Beatrice left the Wheaton farm after delivering the parcel of used clothing that Mrs. Stewart had donated to Maryanne. She directed the horse to the main road and headed back to the Stewart cottage. A small patch of beautiful flowers in the field caught her eye. She stopped and wandered into the meadow to choose a bouquet. The winds picked up with signs of another afternoon rain lurking in the distance.

Beatrice loved flowers and remembered her garden at Grimwald. It served as her only refuge from her abusive husband, Nathan. *Nathan, you miserable beggar, you took my baby boy—my dear sweet Jeremiah.* She approached the flowers taking care not to step on them and looked to the distant village. *Where are you my son?* She wondered if Nathan had poisoned her son against her and if Naomi had contact with her brother.

The dark clouds were approaching very quickly, as were the fateful days ahead. Beatrice was certain that she would be expected to fill the position at Naomi's home. *This is not the reunion that I envisioned with my baby.* She looked forlornly at the waving flowers and chose one. She held it up to enjoy the sweet scent running a finger across the petals.

"So delicate, like my Naomi's feelings..." She questioned Naomi's strength to withstand the strong winds of reality, steadily approaching her world. Beatrice closed her eyes, when a grip on her shoulders startled her.

"I wandered lonely as a cloud
That float on high o'er vales and hills,
When all at once I saw a crowd,
A host of golden daffodils;
Beside the lake, beneath the trees,
Fluttering and dancing in the breeze."

—William Wordsworth

Chapter VI

"The Confession"

"To be really honest means
making confession
whether you can afford it or not,
refusing unmerited praise,
looking painful truths in the face"

—Aubrey De Vere

"Birdy?"

Beatrice swung around to the delightful smile of her dearest friend.

"Daniel!"

She threw her arms around his neck without a thought. Surprised, Daniel reciprocated the embrace. Beatrice pulled back, a little embarrassed by her enthusiasm and Daniel took her hand in his.

"Birdy, I have a matter o' some urgency to discuss wit' ya."

"*Daniel*, your sister, Abigail, is well?"

"Abby is well. Can ya spare me a few minutes?"

"Daniel, I could spare you a lifeti..."

Daniel's brows rose. Beatrice nervously dropped her gaze to the flower.

"I meant to say that I have finished my duties for the day."

"Is there someplace that we might talk? It shall be rainin', soon." Daniel looked to the sky.

"I have very little privacy at the Stewart home."

"We could go to me friend Hiram's estate."

"No! No, not yet," she stammered.

Daniel shifted uneasily. *When shall ya feel safe with me? Shall ya e'er confide in me?*

"Birdy, would ye be up to a ride to Laudershire, the village west o' here?"

Beatrice nodded.

"We can take the wagon back to the Stewart's and use me cart." Daniel offered Beatrice his arm and they returned to the road. When they arrived at the Stewart cottage, Beatrice hurried inside to change her clothes. She met Mrs. Stewart in the hall.

"My friend Daniel has returned. We are going to Laudershire."

"Edward McDonnally paid me a visit while ya were out. Ye shall be cookin' for he and his missus after their weddin' and cleanin' here on Wednesday and Saturday mornin's. Thought ye could be usin' the extra income." Mrs. Stewart continued to the kitchen. The walls seemed to close in around Beatrice. The single flower fell from her hands. Any thought of changing her clothes vanished and she walked to the front door and out onto the porch. Daniel jumped from the cart and ran to her, the moment that he saw her stunned, pale face.

"Birdy, are you ill?" Daniel asked with deep concern.

"No, no…"

Daniel offered his hand and she climbed up and sat down next to him. He took the reins.

"Are ya certain yer up to travelin', Birdy?"

"Yes, I need time to gather my thoughts."

"Daniel nodded and drove the cart toward the village. Neither spoke again until they reached the quaint inn on the village square.

"The food is good here and 'tis quiet," Daniel reported.

Beatrice and Daniel sat down at a table by a window, near the back. Only two other patrons were present.

"Daniel, I cannot eat anything."

"Have ya eaten since this mornin'?"

"No, but—"

"Ya shall be eatin' now. I shan't hear a word about it." When the innkeeper arrived, Daniel ordered scones and tea for them.

"As ya do not feel like talkin', I shall. Birdy, I enjoyed yer letters, more than ya know. I think we are the best o' friends, are we not?"

Beatrice nodded.

"Birdy...I believe that we have been brought together by the hand o' the Almighty to face our troubles together. Ya need to trust me. Ya'll ne'er find a more loyal friend."

Beatrice's eyes welled up. She pulled her hankie from her pocketbook and blotted the escaping tears.

"Ah, Birdy, I ne'er meant to make ya cry."

The innkeeper arrived with their order and Daniel feebly offered an unintentional ironic explanation. "She received a bit o' bad news."

The innkeeper gave Beatrice a sympathetic look and left them to their privacy.

"There is somethin' ye should know," Daniel said reluctantly.

"I apologize, Daniel," she sniffled. "What do you have to tell me?"

"I had a visitor in London."

"Not *Cecil*, Henry's father?" she whispered.

"Nay, a private investigator," Daniel said solemnly.

"Cecil has hired someone to find me?"

Daniel took her hand and shook his head.

"Then who?" she asked anxiously.

"Edward McDonnally."

"Naomi's husband?" she said, appalled, removing her hand from Daniel's.

With her casual reference to Naomi, Daniel stared at her with severity.

"Daniel? Why are you looking at me like that?" Daniel did not answer.

Beatrice proceeded nervously, "I heard recently that Edward and...and his wife, Naomi, are seeking to hire help. Mrs. Stewart told me only today...that he...Mr. McDonnally, paid her a visit. Mrs. Stewart, agreed to have me work for them—Edward and his wife." Beatrice fidgeted with her napkin.

'Tis no wonder that yer upset, Daniel thought.

"Daniel, why are you silent? Actually, I am surprised—no *outraged* that Mr. McDonnally would send an investigator to London to check on me. How *dare* he question my reputation?" Beatrice said indignantly.

Daniel sat studying her face, her resemblance to Naomi and the similar mannerisms.

"Say something, Daniel. Do you not find Mr. McDonnally's behavior in poor taste?"

"Birdy, Edward McDonnally is an honorable man. I have spent many an hour wit' he and Naomi. He only wants the best for her."

"I suppose that it is the usual procedure for the very wealthy...before they bring a stranger into their home," she relented awkwardly.

Daniel waited a few minutes, giving her the opportunity to confess to her relationship with Naomi. It was all for naught.

Daniel leaned back in his chair and folded his hands. He looked her straight in the eye.

"Edward is lookin' for ya. He is plannin' to give ya to Naomi as a weddin' gift," Daniel said cooly, watching for Beatrice's reaction.

She looked away then asked with notable discomfort, "Is it customary to present your wife with a *cook* for a wedding gift?"

"Nay."

She looked confused and disturbed with his reply. Daniel looked at her with disappointment.

"Not a cook...a *mother*, Beatrice MacKenzie."

He pulled out his wallet, threw down a few bills for payment of the meal, pushed his chair from the table and walked out. Beatrice sat stunned, closing her eyes with regret.

How long has he known? Why did he not say something? He must understand why I could not tell him. She looked towards the door.

He expected more from our relationship, more from me—"to face our troubles together", "a more loyal friend"... he was waiting for me to confess and I failed him.

She picked up her pocketbook, left the table and walked over to the door. Daniel was sitting on a bench on the green across the road. Beatrice had never met a man like Daniel and felt the odds were against her meeting another like him.

You think that I am spineless, unappreciative, and unworthy of your friendship, she thought and set out to prove that he was mistaken. She walked across the road and stood before him. He looked up with surprise to see her intense expression.

"Daniel O'Leardon, I am Beatrice Smithfield MacKenzie. Naomi, Jeremiah and Henry are my children," her voice cracked. "I left Grimwald and my detestable husband, abandoning my baby, Jeremiah, in order to protect Naomi. We moved to Newcastle where after witnessing a horrendous crime, I was kidnapped...I gave birth to my son, Henry. Years later, I finally got the courage to leave." She wiped the tears from her cheeks. "I thank God, that he presented me with a guardian angel, the most incredible man in the world, who gave me friendship and hope."

Daniel's heart melted. He stood up to comfort her.

Beatrice stepped back to continue. "No, let me finish. And...I think it is only appropriate at this time to inform you that I agree—we *were* brought together by divine providence to face our troubles together. *And*, whether you approve or not, I love you with all my heart and soul and despite how angry you are with me, you had better learn to live with it because..." she sniffled, "from this day forward, I do not intend to live another day of my life without you. And yes, Edward McDonnally shall have his wedding gift."

Daniel was blushing and speechless.

"Mr. O'Leardon, do you not think that this would be a good time to kiss me, so that I know that I have not made a bloomin' fool of myself?" she said with fearful eyes.

Daniel shyly cocked his head and smiled the sweetest smile, she had ever seen.

"Aye, Birdy."

That afternoon, the innkeeper, the two patrons at the inn, three passing residents and a stray dog witnessed one of history's most romantic moments.

In London, Mr. Jorgensen, Edward's hired investigator, had put together the puzzling pieces of the location of Naomi's mother, Beatrice, and planned to return to Lochmoor and report his findings.

Later that day, Daniel and Beatrice devised a plan to deliver "Edward's wedding gift" without his knowledge—which meant intercepting the return of Edward's investigator. The scheme depended on the absolute discretion and cooperation of several trustworthy residents of Lochmoor. The minute Mr. Jorgensen reached the outskirts of the village, he was escorted to the Kilvert cottage and convinced to withhold any information of Beatrice's where-abouts while their plan was set into motion. Their plan also heavily relied on Harriet Dugan's reputation as the village gossip. Within an hour, the rumor that a very important guest would accompany Daniel O'Leardon to Edward and Naomi's wedding, successfully spread through Lochmoor Glen and several surrounding villages. The rumor stirred the imaginations of members of every walk of life with their predictions ranging from the possibilities of the arrival of a famous poet to an enchanting member of royalty.

No one found the news of Daniel's guest more captivating than McDonnally Manor's housekeeper, and Daniel's first love, Eloise. The day before the wedding, Eloise's curiosity consumed her sub-conscience.

"Eloise, would you please hand me the place cards?" Naomi asked.

"Place cards?"

"Yes, the gold ones on the breakfront."

"What are you going to do with them, mum?"

"Place them, of course."

"Where, mum?"

"On the *table*. Now, let me see, who shall sit here?"

"Mum, I can do this for you."

"Now Eloise, this has to be perfect." Naomi shuffled through the cards. "Edward and I shall be at the head and Hiram and Abigail opposite us, for balance. Daniel shall desire to speak with Hiram, so I shall put him on his—no, I think we need a man, woman, pattern. We can place Daniel's guest on Hiram's left. But, what if it is a gentleman poet? There goes the pattern," Naomi fretted. "Well, no matter, we shall put the mystery guest on Hiram's left. Daniel can sit next to Abigail. Sophia shall desire to converse with both Abigail and Daniel. She can sit next to Daniel. Perfect! See how very simple this is, Eloise?"

Naomi positioned herself on the other side of the table. Rahzvon shall have to sit next to Sophia. Oh, dear, who is going to sit next to Daniel's poet? It has to be a woman. Allison. No, if this poet is handsome, Guillaume shall be irate."

"That is certain," Eloise agreed.

"Very well, Eloise, you shall have to do the honors."

"But Mum, I *cannot*," Eloise objected adamantly.

"Yes, I insist. You love poetry. You have a wealth of subjects to discuss."

"But, what if it is not a poet. It may be a woman or a glamorous princess. I am but a housemaid," Eloise pleaded.

"Not on my wedding day—you are a dear friend." Naomi looked over to see Eloise sprawled out in one of the chairs. "Eloise?"

"I am not feeling well."

"Eloise, is it Daniel's guest? Are you feeling freckleswept again?"

Eloise wrung her hands.

"No, mum, I have *just...* never seen Daniel with anyone."

"It may be no one—a fellow bookworm." Naomi sat down next to Eloise. "Life is strange, is it not, Eloise?"

"Yes, it is," Eloise sighed.

"When I arrived in Lochmoor, I had hopes that Hiram and I could work out our differences. I would soon become the Mistress of McDonnally Manor. Now, Abigail is destined for that honor."

"Do you regret that, mum?"

"Definitely not. Had Hiram and I reunited, I doubt that McDonnally Manor would still be standing," Naomi laughed.

"With Miss O'Leardon, it may not last long either."

"Yes, it takes a woman with a strong constitution to tame Hiram. They are a fearsome match. *I* do well to maintain a friendship with him." Naomi stood. "Now, no more about it. Come upstairs, I need to try on my dress. Did Albert bring my trunk from the manor house?"

"Yes, mum."

Naomi took Eloise's arm to go up to the bedroom to make the final alterations for the wedding gown.

That evening, Edward chose to work on his stamp album, to calm his wedding jitters, when he gave notice to a slight tapping at the library window behind him. He stared, momentarily, at the pane, then with the aid of his magnifying lens, resumed his observation of a newly acquired stamp.

A second tapping led him to investigate. He lifted the sash and leaned out, craning in every direction to see the source of the annoyance. One last look towards the barn ended with a tug on his collar and a swift pull on his belt from behind. Ten seconds later, the groom of the next day found himself at the mercy of a half dozen men armed with pails of soot. Edward closed his eyes, feeling very much the fool while his abductors made an effort to cover his body with soot, from head to toe. There was no sense in fighting tradition and Edward knew it. His captors pulled him into the wagon and drove him off to the village square.

In reaching the outskirts, Jake Kilvert, the postman's son, called out to the others, now laughing uncontrollably. "Men, the creel is ready!"

The Master of McDonnally Manor received the honor of tying the stone-filled basket to his uncle's back. "Dear uncle, 'tis a wee burden you bear in comparison to that of married life. And it shall strengthen that leg of yours!" Hiram laughed.

"Remember this day, Hiram. It is looming nearer and nearer for you, old man," Edward cautioned.

"Aye, but I shall not be so foolish in opening the window to fall prey to this abuse."

For the next twenty minutes, Edward paraded through the square, accompanied by heckling and cries of his arrival. The merry band of village men and the captive groom returned to the wagon to drive Edward back to his home. There, they dropped him and drove off. Several minutes later, Rahzvon returned. He walked over to Edward, brooding on the lawn to untie the basket from his back.

"Sir, your nephew instructed me, of course without knowledge to the rest of the party, to escort you to your barn."

Edward looked very suspiciously at the messenger.

"Come, along." Rahzvon lifted the creel as though it were empty and helped the tired filthy groom to the barn.

"You too, lad are in line for this traitorous treachery," Edward warned.

"No, sir, I am not a Scot."

"Aye, but as they say, when in Rome..."

Rahzvon shuddered at the thought.

The quaint sight of the stall equipped with two burning oil lamps, a steaming bath and a small table laden with a fresh towel, a clean set of clothes and a new western novel greeted them.

Edward could not refrain from smiling.

"This is better." He picked up the note on the table. "My nephew is already seeking an ally." Edward read the note to Rahzvon.

"*Keep this in mind, when the tables are turned, your loyal nephew, Hiram.*" Edward chuckled. "You may go now, Mr. Sierzik. I thank you from the bottom of my sooty boots." Edward gave a short bow.

"Good night, sir. Sleep, well."

"I shall if it does not take half the night to remove this," he looked at his soot-covered hands.

While Edward soaked, the bride and the women folk gathered in the McDonnally Manor parlor. Naomi, too, enjoyed the soothing comfort of warm water, with her feet immersed in a small tub. Eloise removed her wedding band and dropped it into the basin. As each friend customarily washed the bride's feet, she searched for the wedding band. A surprise to all, Sophia found it, signifying that she was next in line for matrimonial bliss.

Naomi detected Abigail's disappointment with the results.

"Abigail, I understand that we should be offering you a round of congratulations for your future as Mrs. McDonnally, as well!"

All the guests immediately offered their good wishes, welcoming Abigail to the community.

Getting back to the matters at hand, Harriet asked, "Do ya hae evr'y thing in order, Naomi?"

"Edward nearly forgot to give the fourteen day notice to the reverend," Naomi reported.

"Ah, forgot the marriage banns?" Harriet gasped.

"Eloise did you press the MacKenzie and McDonnally plaids to hang at the door of the ballroom?"

"The tartans are ready, mum."

"Sophia, did you tell Rahzvon to get the grey horse from the Kilvert's?"

"I did, not to worry."

"Something borrowed, mother! We forgot!" Allison exclaimed.

Sophia interjected, "I have something."

"What is it dear?" Naomi asked.

"My grandmother Amanda's locket, uncle had the ring repaired on it."

"Sophia...how awfully sweet of you. I shall return it to you immediately after the reception. Thank you." Naomi gave her a hug.

"Dunna forget the drop o' blood, "Mrs. Kilvert reminded.

"I really do not think that is necessary," Naomi gave an objectionable frown.

"Mummy, it is only a drop. One tiny prick to the finger and you shall be blessed with good fortune."

Harriet spoke up immediately, "Aye ye best be careful, Maryanne Wheaton was so jittery, she pricked herself too hard and nearly bled all o'er her weddin' dress. She rinsed it and tried ev'ry concoction for removin' it. She ended up hidin' the spot wit' whitewash!"

Naomi wrinkled her nose at the thought.

"I am awfully disappointed that Maryanne could not join us tonight," Naomi said drying her feet and putting on her shoes.

"She is not up to any extras if she is to attend the weddin' tomorrow," Harriet pointed out.

Naomi slid the basin under her chair.

"I miss her, but it is a small sacrifice to have her present for our wedding. Maryanne is such a caring woman and so busy with the children and the farm. Oh, thank you, for offering to pick up the flowers with Rahzvon, tomorrow, Sophia."

"Trust me. The pleasure shall be most definitely mine," Sophia affirmed.

"Aye, if I were but one and twenty, I too, would be countin' the minutes 'til that wee jaunt wit' the eye catchin' Mr. Sierzik," Harriet laughed.

"Now, Naomi, remember tomorrow—do not look in the mirror, once you are fully dressed," Abigail warned.

"I shan't," Naomi vowed.

After much giggling and another hour of conversation and refreshments, the party disbanded. Naomi walked up to retire to the guest room on the second floor of McDonnally Manor for the last time.

Chapter VII

"Horse of A.."

"For a tender beaming smile
To my hope has been granted,
And tomorrow she shall hear
All my fond heart say."

—Samuel Ferguson

Sophia sat next to Rahzvon, watching him handle the reins with ease. Driving had never been of any particular concern to her in the past when riding with Albert or Guillaume, but with Rahzvon, his every movement sparked her interest. Sophia desired to learn every detail of his character—his strengths and his weaknesses. She watched his effortless and natural control of the horses as he hastened their pace. She slid her arm around his and smiled. The muggy air caressed her face as she brushed back the uncooperative curls framing it. Rahzvon kept his eyes to the road, alerted to the menacing ruts and potholes.

"Rahzvon?"

"Yes, Phia?"

"Do you long to return to your country?"

"I try to preoccupy myself with more pleasant thoughts." He snapped the reins and Duff moved out. "Are you missing Paris, Phia?"

"No, but I do miss my mother."

"If I had the means, I would take you there. Family is important."

"I appreciate the thought. There is no one I would rather have accompany me to France."

"I am not certain of that. I am no match for your thrill-seeking shopping companion."

"Abigail?"

"Now, Phia, you have to admit that Miss O'Leardon would be more agreeable for a tour of the Paris shops."

"A holiday with Abigail would no doubt be absolutely sweet, but it would pale in comparison to returning home on the arm of a handsome gentleman such as yourself," Sophia smiled.

Rahzvon moved the reins to one hand and with the other, gently squeezed her arm in appreciation.

"Besides, Abigail would never leave my uncle," Sophia added.

They arrived at the Wheaton farm and pulled into the lane leading to the house. Jeanie Wheaton shot out of the front door ecstatic to greet her hero.

"Master Rahzfun! Master Rahzfun!"
Sophia and Rahzvon exchanged grins with Jeanie's mispronunciation.

"Good morning, Jeanie," Rahzvon returned.

Jeanie's little legs delivered her to the cart in seconds.

"How are you today, Miss?" Rahzvon asked.

Jeanie climbed up into the cart with the aid of Sophia's hand.

"Verra well, sir. Hullo, Miss Donnally," Jeanie said as she squeezed between Sophia and Rahzvon. Jeanie latched onto Rahzvon's arm and looked up to him with adoring eyes.

"Master Rahzfun, I hae been thinking 'bout climbin' again."

"You have?" Rahzvon answered with surprise.

"Aye, sir. Ye may hafta save me again," Jeanie said seriously.

"I think you better keep those pretty shoes planted safely on the ground," Rahzvon suggested.

"Sir, me shoes, pretty? They were Corinne's."

"That is exactly why they are so beautiful."

"I dunna understand."

"Is not Corinne the perfect picture of health?" Rahzvon asked.

Jeanie looked toward the house where Corinne sat on the step.

Rahzvon explained, "Those shoes have served her well, and now they shall do the same for you. Thus, they are quite to my liking. You should feel proud to wear them."

Jeanie looked down at her feet swinging freely in front of her, evaluating the footwear with skepticism. She looked to Sophia, also examining the small scuffed shoes; then to her hero.

"I shall wear 'em 'cause ya like 'em and 'cause they're the only ones I hae."

Rahzvon placed his arm around her small shoulders and gave Jeanie a comforting hug.

"Now, Miss Wheaton, could you, please, do me a favor and ask your mother as to where we are to find the flowers?"

"I can show ye. That way to the barn." Jeanie pointed.

"As you say." Rahzvon urged Duff down the road.

When they reached the barn, Jeanie directed them to the left to a small white out-building with hazy multi-paned windows.

"They're in there," Jeanie announced.

Rahzvon pulled the cart around to park. He climbed down and lifted Jeanie to the ground.

"Thank ye, sir," Jeanie said latching on to his coattail.

"You are quite welcome," he added as he helped Sophia down.

"I am grateful, as well, *sir*," Sophia added.

Jeanie clutched Rahzvon's hand and led him to the failing greenhouse. Sophia followed close behind.

When they entered the building, Sophia noted, admiring a dozen bouquets arranged in jars on the long, wooden table, "Oh, Rahzvon, they are beautiful."

"Yes, I do not know much about flowers, but I am certain the McDonnallys will be pleased. Your mother should feel very proud," Rahzvon commented while draining most of the water from one of the jars.

"Proud, like me, wit' me shoes?" Jeanie asked.

"Yes, Jeanie," Rahzvon gave a loving pat on her head.

"I shall fetch the crate from the cart," Sophia said carrying the drained vase of flowers; Rahzvon proceeded to drain the other jars to prepare them for their journey.

"Master Rahzfun?"

"Yes, Jeanie?"

"Could ye take me to the weddin'?"

"Jeanie, I am certain that your mother is planning for you to accompany her and your sisters—especially, with your father away."

"I dunna think me mother is goin'," she said confidently.

"*Jeanie*," Rahzvon looked down at her suspiciously, "of course she is. Your mother has spent the last week preparing for the McDonnally wedding, making special dresses for you and your sisters."

Jeanie pulled a wooden box over to the table. She climbed onto it and stood up next to him. Now, at a more desirable height, at the level of Rahzvon's chest, Jeanie peered up with a hopeful gaze. Sophia approached the doorway in time to witness the conversation.

"Sir, why did ya rescue me?"

"Because you are a wonderful little girl and I did not want you to be harmed."

Jeanie's head lowered while she mumbled, "Do ye love me wit' all yer heart?"

Rahzvon sat down the last jar in surprise to the unexpected inquiry.

Sophia listened intently, curious as to how Rahzvon would respond, knowing care must be taken with Jeanie's innocent naivety.

"With all my heart?" he asked gently.

"That is what me father says to me mother," she answered with a mature tone.

"Your parents have known each other for a very long time, Jeanie," Rahzvon explained nervously, trying to avoid hurting his five-year old admirer.

"I hae known ye for a verra long time," Jeanie reminded. "Ye do love me?" she asked with worry.

"Why yes, Jeanie."

Jeanie sighed with relief. Her tiny arms embraced Rahzvon, while Sophia stood behind them with a wide grin, shaking her head. Jeanie looked up at Rahzvon, and indicated with her thumb and index finger.

"I grew this much, since summer."

"That is great, Jeanie."

"It willna be only a few more summers, then I shall be tall and we shall hae a weddin'!"

Rahzvon's eyes widened and his smile faded. Sophia covered her mouth to hide her amusement. Rahzvon peered down at the little glowing face before him, uncomfortably anticipating her reaction if he dashed her hopes of becoming Mrs. Sierzik. Sophia considered intervening to assist, but chose to remain silent.

"Jeanie, I shall be an old man, by the time you are ready to marry," Rahzvon said compassionately.

"I willna mind. I shall look after ye. I can knit ye a shawl like ol' Mr. Cummin' wears. I shall learn to knit verra soon, Mama told me! Marvel can knit and she is but eight years old!"

Rahzvon lifted Jeanie to the ground and avoided any further discussion of the matter by abruptly changing the subject.

"We had better get moving along." He picked up two vases and turned to leave, finding himself face to face with "the other woman". Sophia whispered as he passed, "Not unlike my uncle's plight, you attract women like bees to honey."

"Bees produce the honey," Rahzvon contradicted.

"And you, sir, have produced yours," Sophia teased as she handed a jar to Jeanie, confused by the comment.

"Careful now, Jeanie," Sophia instructed.

Jeanie and Sophia followed Rahzvon to the cart with the remaining bouquets. He placed them in the crate and stuffed the flower sacks around the jars to hold them in place.

"I am going up to the house to thank Mrs. Wheaton," Sophia said.

"Better show her the way, Jeanie," Rahzvon insisted preventing any further conversation on his marital plans.

Jeanie returned an endearing smile and took Sophia's hand. Sophia entered the Wheaton home surprised to find Mrs. Wheaton, looking poorly, sitting in the rocking chair. The eldest daughter, Wilmoth, was ironing one of the dresses for the wedding.

"Hello, Mrs. Wheaton... Are you ill?" Sophia asked with concern.

"Only a wee tired, Miss McDonnally. Me girls are a big help, and soon their father shall return from the hospital."

Sophia nodded sympathetically. "We appreciate the flowers, they are lovely. Here is the payment." She pulled a roll of bills from her skirt pocket.

Mrs. Wheaton took it and replied, "'Tis too much."

"No, Naomi insisted. You raise the loveliest flowers in the village."

"Ye thank her for me, Miss McDonnally."

"I shall. Now, can I help in anyway?"

"Me four older girls are bathed and the dresses are pressed. Might ye fetch me daughters and take 'em to the weddin'? I am not certain that I shall be gettin' there on time."

Jeanie gave a knowing grin.

"Certainly, Mrs. Wheaton. I shall ask Rahzvon to come for them in a few hours."

Jeanie listened attentively to Sophia's pronunciation of Rahzvon's name.

"Are you certain, that I cannot help in some way?" Sophia said with concern.

"Nay, takin' 'em is all I would be needin."

"Very well, we shall be going now. Thank you again and take care, Mrs. Wheaton."

"Good day, Miss McDonnally."

"Good day."

Jeanie escorted Sophia out to the cart.

"Master Rahzfu...Rahz...von, I shall be seeing ye verra soon in my bonnie new dress."

"I am looking forward to it." Rahzvon waved.

"Good bye, Miss Donnally," Jeanie said with little enthusiasm.

"See you soon, Jeanie," Sophia waved as the cart moved towards the main road.

"Mrs. Wheaton asked if we could arrange for the girls to be driven to the wedding. Would you mind, Rahzvon?"

"No, I shall drive them."

"Mrs. Wheaton appears to be exhausted, she has taken on too many responsibilities," Sophia said sympathetically.

"She has very little choice in the matter, with little money and her husband absent. I promise to never leave you in a similar situation," Rahzvon looked intently to Sophia.

"You need not worry about me, Mr. Sierzik. I am certain that *my* husband shall adequately provide for me," she said coyly.

"Your husband?" Rahzvon asked, scowling.

"Yes, you certainly do not plan on being a bigamist, do you? The future Jeanie Sierzik would surely not approve."

"Your humor is not welcome, Sophia."

"Rahzvon, you take everything so seriously."

I do? He smiled to himself.

"She is but a five-year old child who has fallen for the man who saved her life," Sophia explained.

"Yes, but that man does not want to break her heart."

Sophia snuggled close to him, admiring his sense of compassion and offered no further comment on that subject.

"The horse, Rahzvon? Did you get the horse, this morning?" Sophia asked casually.

"What horse?"

"*What horse*? The grey one from Mr. Kilvert's brother!" she panicked.

"Why do you need another horse? There are plenty of horses to go around."

"Rahzvon, are you saying that you did not get it?" Sophia screeched. "We need it to pull the wedding carriage!"

"Why would do you need that old nag when you have Duff? He is quite handsome."

"Can you not follow the simplest of instructions? It has to be a *grey* horse!"

"Instructions? You never mentioned anything about a horse."

"I certainly did!"

"*When*?"

"When you and Jake were ridiculing my poor uncle, who *suffered* from your antics, last evening!"

"I never heard you say anything of the kind, Phia."

"A typical distracted male, never hears but what he wants to hear! Now what are we to do? We have to get that grey horse! I promised Naomi."

Rahzvon pulled the wagon into the drive of the McDonnally estate leading to the back gate and stopped.

"Phia, why does it have to be a grey horse?"

"It is good luck for the marriage. If you would listen once in a while we would not be in this sticky wicket!"

"If it is mandatory that we get this horse, we can pick it up on the way to the Wheaton farm to get the girls."

"Rahzvon, the Kilvert farm is on the other side of the village." She moved in close to him with a demanding stare, "I cannot let Naomi down, especially on her wedding day. Rahzvon, this is serious!" She climbed down from the wagon.

"Does anyone other than Mr. Kilvert have a grey one?"

"Such an *original* idea, Rahzvon," she said sarcastically. You are truly amazing."

"I know."

Sophia rolled her eyes and leaned against the wagon, brooding. "Rahzvon this is serious."

"*Everything* is serious with you."

"I let Naomi down, as well as everyone in the clan. I should leave Lochmoor. Everyone shall blame me for *your* mistake. They shall have me removed from the clan for spoiling the wedding," she pouted.

Rahzvon walked behind her and smoothed her hair with his hand.

"Phia, I apologize. I realize now, how important this is to you. I admire you for your sense of responsibility to your family. Forgive me, even if it is a silly superstition."

Sophia said nothing. Rahzvon looked toward the horse.

"Phia! I have it—I shall get your grey horse. Come with me." He unhitched Duff.

"Where?" she took his hand.

"To the barn."

"To the barn? There are no grey horses in the barn."

"There soon shall be," Rahzvon led the way.

When they entered, Rahzvon explained, "Watch this." He ran over to the bench beneath the tack rack and pulled out the tin with the soot used to christen the groom. He peered into the can, "Not too much left, but I wager enough to do the job."

"You are daft, Rahzvon. Your life shall be worth nothing if you so much as touch Uncle's prize Hannoverian with that…"

"What choice do we have, your uncle's momentary wrath or a lifetime of doom for the bride and groom?" Rahzvon laughed, "Clever rhyme, hey?"

"Clever," she repeated, failing to see the humor.

"And what would the wedding be without Duff in attendance? He is part of the clan. Observe closely, Miss McDonnally." He pulled a pair of work gloves from a basket on the floor.

"After this, I shan't be a McDonnally for long," Sophia lamented.

Rahzvon turned with one gloved hand in the soot and paused, "You do not desire to remain a McDonnally forever, do you?" he said with a sly grin.

Sophia was glued to her position, thinking, *No, you know I do not. How is it that even when you vex me the most, you manage to turn everything around with your charm?*

She gave a short sigh. *There is my answer,* she looked at his ever-so-appealing appearance. "Very well, I shall help."

Rahzvon handed her a pair of gloves, tore a scrap from the cloth from the grooming chest and prepared it for her. They proceeded to Duff's stall and began the application in a circular motion, soothing the beautiful, white giant.

After they added the finishing touches to Duff, Sophia and Rahzvon dressed for the wedding and drove the carriage to the Wheaton farm.

"Willmuff, look, Duff's an ol' man!" Jeanie called from the front porch.

"Miss McDonnally," Wilmoth shouted, "what happened to Duff?"

Sophia turned to Rahzvon and smirked.

"What makes you think this is Duff?" Rahzvon asked.

"Ye canna fool me," Jeanie sniggered pointing at Duff's brand.

"Never you mind, little lassie, we need to get to the church."

Maryanne gave a weak smile and sent her four daughters off with a kiss. Rahzvon began lifting them into the back of the wagon, one-by-one onto the woolen blanket.

"I want to sit by you, mum," Jeanie begged.

I know better, little miss, Sophia thought as she scooted next to Rahzvon and took his arm. "You are fine where you are, Jeanie. The ride shall be brief."

"Behave now! I love ya!" Maryanne waved as the cart moved out onto the road from the lane.

"I canna sit here!" Corinne screamed.

Sophia turned to see Corinne standing. "Sit down Corinne!"

"No!"

"Rahzvon, please stop the wagon," Sophia insisted.

Rahzvon halted Duff and Sophia turned to Corinne.

"She canna sit or she shall be gettin' the rash," Marvel explained.

"Wool gives her the rash," Wilmoth reiterated.

"Who ever heard of a Scot having a problem with wool," Rahzvon teased.

"I say, 'tis true," Corinne defended.

"We believe you, Corinne. You may sit up here with us." Sophia helped her to the seat.

Jeanie popped up immediately.

"Look at me legs, red as beets! Me legs itch all over," Jeanie whined, hoping to snag the opportunity to sit next to the handsome Mr. Sierzik.

Sophia knitted her brows skeptically.

"Dunna listen to her, she wears wool stockin's all the time," Wilmoth contradicted.

Sophia ignored Jeanie's complaints. "Jeanie, please sit down next to Marvel, we are running late."

Jeanie scowled, pouting with jealousy, and dropped to the wagon bed.

"Hold on, ladies," Rahzvon warned as he encouraged Duff.

Before long, the melodious song of Joseph Dugan's bagpipes met them when they reached the outskirts of the village. Marvel and Wilmoth giggled with excitement as they checked their hair bows for precise positioning. Jeanie remained in a huff between them.

Chapter VIII

"The Ceremony"

"And ye shall seek me,
And find me, when ye search
for me with all your heart."

—Jeremiah 29:13

Down the road at McDonnally Manor, Edward and Hiram sat in the guest room. They were in full Highland dress.

"After last night's escapades, you owe me, my dear nephew," Edward reprimanded.

"I owe you? Have you forgotten the meeting that you arranged for me with Miss Nettlepin?"

"Ah, yes the breath-taking schoolmarm. Hiram, I cannot imagine that you were at all surprised to have her swooning over you. She may not be every man's ideal, but she is a woman."

"That is debatable; one would describe her more accurately as an octopus with spectacles."

"Without spectacles," Edward corrected. "Did you inform Abigail of Miss Nettlepin's hospitality?"

"No, I did not. Lochmoor Glen may be temporarily without a schoolhouse, but there is no need for the village to lose its only teacher, as well."

"Aye, Abigail has little tolerance for the members of her sex fawning over you. Naomi has the same difficulty with me." Edward said jokingly. He looked in the mirror to admire his truly Scottish appearance. "Not to change this fascinating subject, but I must say that I did appreciate the eloquent bathing arrangements in the barn. I shall remember to do the same for you."

"Ah, but I am a young lad of thirty-five. I need not commit until I am at least as old as you are," Hiram grinned.

"Abigail may have a slight objection to an engagement as long as that, but your postponement would be a significant contribution to society. Imagine all of those women, all of those Miss Nettlepins who would enjoy another eight years dreaming of becoming the Mistress of

McDonnally Manor," Edward said with mock reverence.

"Indeed." Hiram straightened his kilt. "No, I may not marry Abigail tomorrow, but I daresay that I cherish the thought of calling her my wife."

"I foresee a capital future for the four of us, Hiram. We shall have a grand time, if I can get past today and my knees stop shaking."

Hiram patted Edward's shoulder.

"It shan't be the last time that you shall be a bundle of nerves, Edward, if you are to fill the rooms of Brachney Hall with wee McDonnallys. Not to worry, I shall join you in the pacing with every bairn."

"Abigail may bless you with a half dozen children, as well, Hiram."

"Abby and I shan't have children, we shall have *wildcats*."

Edward laughed at the image.

Then the room fell silent and Edward looked to his nephew with genuine appreciation.

"Hiram, although the years have brought a great deal of pain and suffering, I feel I can speak freely with you," Edward said solemnly.

"Aye?" Hiram asked nervously, expecting a comment pertaining to Naomi, Hiram's first love.

"*Who* is Daniel bringing to the wedding? I am going batty with curiosity."

Hiram shook his head, "I have no information to offer. You know as much as I."

"I heard that it may be a Spanish dancer or an eccentric actress from the theatre," Edward said with child-like enthusiasm.

"With Daniel, anything is possible." *The woman at the Stewart home?*

The grandfather clock chimed in the hall.

"It shan't be long before the mystery is solved, Uncle. We had better make haste. Mrs. Edward McDonnally is waiting to make this marriage official."

In the Brachney Hall drawing room, Allison placed the last pin in the bride's hair while Eloise tied a plaid ribbon around the bouquet.

"Beautiful, Mother. Positively perfection. You look like a princess." Abigail glowed.

Naomi stared off into space, realizing that she may not look like a princess, but she was the spittin' image of her mother, as she remembered her. Her thoughts flashed back to the London shop and the encounter with the man who she believed may possibly be a half-brother.

How I do wish Vivian would have sent favorable news, Naomi thought with disappointment in not receiving the letter from the store clerk which verified her suspicions. Naomi turned to her daughter and back to the present.

"Thank you, Baby, for your assistance. I wonder how the prince is faring."

"Ask Eloise, I am going to run and check on Guillaume, in the kitchen. I am keeping a close eye on him, since Miss Dunmore arrived. I shall be back to join you in the ballroom for that final check," Allison said in passing Eloise in the hall.

"Hello, Eloise, how is the groom?" Naomi inquired.

"Hello, Mum. Albert said that he has a severe case of nerves."

"As he should, it is not every day that a man marries his wife," Naomi laughed.

"Indeed not. Mum, how are you doing?"

"Perfectly, except for the pin prick." Naomi examined her finger.

"You seem a bit preoccupied since you returned from London."

"You never miss a trick, do you, Eloise? I do have more on my mind than the wedding. I met someone in London...a gentleman."

"Mum?" Eloise gave Naomi a worrisome look.

"No, no, he was someone who I thought may be a relative."

"*May be?*" Eloise asked.

"Before I had a chance to ask him, he had vanished," Naomi explained.

"I am at a loss, Mum." Baffled, Eloise shook her head.

"It is of no consequence. I have all the friends and family that I need to have the perfect wedding. I am so happy that my brother, Jeremiah, is coming."

"When do you expect him, Mum?"

"He said that he shall drive directly to the church. He has a new motorcar."

"There goes the reception," Eloise said with despair.

"What are you implying?"

"Mum, every man in the village shall be outside, gawking at the motorcar instead of visiting in the ballroom."

"Eloise, your insight is *remarkable*. I am going to leave word for Jeremiah to leave it parked in the village. Albert can drive him from the church."

"I shall tell Albert."

"Tell him not to breathe a word about the motorcar, Eloise."

"Yes, Mum."

"Now, I must make that final check of the ballroom before we leave."

"Mind your dress and walk slowly so you shan't perspire," Eloise suggested.

"I am back, Mother," Allison called from the hall.

Mother, daughter and the trailing Patience arrived at the door to the ballroom located on the fourth floor. Despite Eloise's warning, the half-winded women arrived at the gaily-decorated room. The tables wore matching linen and the aroma of Maryanne's bouquets filled the air. Refreshment tables were prepared with crystal, fine china and silver to accommodate the guests. A small area adjacent to the veranda was roped off for the musicians. Naomi ran her fingers over the leather bound guest book, which lay waiting on a small stand by the door. Her eyes welled up as she lifted Patience to her arms.

"Edward was right when he said that all I needed was 'patience.' It is no longer a dream, Allison."

"Now, Mummy, no tears. Save those for the ceremony."

Naomi looked over the room. "The staff did an excellent job. Shall we go?" She placed the cat on the floor. "I shall be back, Patience, as the new Mistress of Brachney Hall."

The two hustled down the stairs and met Eloise in the hall.

"Mother, do you have everything?"

"Yes, I put a new silver coin in my shoe, for the 'something new'."

"Are you wearing the blue garter?" Eloise asked.

"Yes."

"That qualifies for the 'something blue'. It was awfully nice of Sophia to think of loaning you Amanda's locket, since we did not have something old from your mo–" Allison stopped fearfully.

"Yes, I know, Allison... We did not have something old from the *mother* of the bride. I may not have *my* mother present, but God willing, I shall be there for you on your wedding day."

"I know, Mummy," Allison said tenderly and gave Naomi a hug.

Thinking about its origin, Naomi reached up and caressed the locket hanging from her neck. *Uncanny, if I had married Hiram, I may have worn this locket then, as well.* Naomi put her arm lovingly around Allison's shoulders, remembering the painful conflict they experienced over Hiram.

"Oh, Mother!" Allison scolded. "You were to step out the door with your right foot, first."

Naomi stepped back into the hall and made a second attempt to satisfy the superstition.

The three women rushed out to the carriage and climbed in. Eloise pulled in Naomi's train and they were off. The ladies were giddy with excitement, chatting a mile a minute until they reached the village. Albert drove the carriage around to the back entrance of the church and parked next to Edward's carriage. Allison and Eloise joined the bride in the backroom.

The church was blooming with the satin bows adorning the pews. There were flowers and lighted candles in every corner. The congregation of Lochmoor residents was bustling with conversation of local gossip and predictions for the renewing marriage. Shortly thereafter, Daniel and Beatrice arrived at the back entrance.

"I shall be returnin' in a minute, Birdy," Daniel said as he climbed down from his carriage. "Shall ye be all right?"

"Yes. Please hurry, Daniel."

Daniel patted her hand and then entered the backdoor. He heard Naomi's voice in the left chamber and turned to the room on the right. Daniel knocked gently. Hiram invited him in.

"Daniel, good to see you." Edward stood and shook his hand.

"A fine woman, yer takin' for yer wife...again. Congratulations."

"Thank you, Daniel."

"Hiram, might I speak wit' ye privately for a minute?"

"Certainly. Please excuse us, Edward," Hiram agreed and stepped out in the hall with his friend and closed the door.

Edward fretted on the other side, convinced that Daniel was revealing information about the mysterious guest.

"Hiram, about me guest... I think I should be presentin' her to the bride and groom before the ceremony."

"Daniel, that is not at all necessary. This is *their* day."

"Trust me, man, it *is* necessary," Daniel said adamantly.

"But Daniel—"

"Hiram, ye know me better than any man in this world, I would ne'er insist if it were not extremely important."

"But Naomi shan't agree to have Edward see her before the ceremony. She nearly suffered heart failure when Edward opened the door when she arrived."

"Ah, I forgot." Daniel stood looking confused. "I fear it shall be disastrous," Daniel's face reddened.

"Daniel, *who* have you invited?" Hiram raised his voice a notch.

"Shh! Keep yer voice down. Not a more welcome guest, I promise ya. I shall have to take her into the church now, she is waitin'," Daniel said with frustration.

"Who is she, Daniel? Is it the woman employed at the Stewart farm?" Hiram whispered.

"Ye shall see." Daniel left out the backdoor. Hiram stood perplexed.

"Oh, my dear friend, what have you done?" He rushed to the door and watched as the carriage disappeared around the corner of the church.

Hiram rejoined the groom.

"Well, man, who is it?" Edward asked impatiently.

"A woman. Someone favorable and of extreme importance, I believe," Hiram stood pondering.

"Royalty, Hiram?"

"He did not say. It is of no consequence now. Let us makes sure that everything is first class," he said straightening Edward's jacket.

Edward then dropped back to the chair and rested his head in his hands.

"Hiram, I *am* getting married," he said dazed.

"Aye, and not a better man deserves such an honor. Naomi *is* royalty."

Daniel helped the beautifully dressed, nervous, mother-of-the-bride from his carriage.

"Birdy, I have ne'er felt more proud than on this day. Ye are as handsome as the bride."

"Thank you, Daniel, for the new clothing and making this all possible. I only hope that we have made the right decision."

"We hae, I feel it in me heart. I am right by yer side and shan't leave it—except for one more minute when I go in and fetch Jeremiah."

"Thank you, Daniel."

The guests were silent now, listening to the pipes playing when Daniel opened the church doors. The crowd was shocked to see Daniel alone, as all were anticipating the arrival of the mysterious guest. Daniel moved quickly to the front pew.

"Jeremiah?" Daniel addressed the young man.

"Aye, sir."

"I am Daniel O'Leardon, a friend of the bride and groom. Could you please accompany me for a minute?"

Jeremiah nodded. Daniel led the way to the church doors, praying that the meeting would go well. He took a deep breath when he opened the doors. Joseph silenced his pipes.

"Jeremiah, may I present—" Daniel began.

Jeremiah immediately recognized the familiarity of the face so similar to his sister's.

"Mother?" Jeremiah stood stunned and confused.

Beatrice did not move, lost in the admiration of the handsome man her son had become and fearfully awaiting his response. Daniel quickly placed a protective arm around her waist. She began to tremble with Jeremiah's marked hesitation.

"I am so sorry," Beatrice burst out and cried into her hands.

Jeremiah compassionately observed the mother he had never known. He was aware of her inexplicable disappearance and the unlikely possibility of it being voluntary. He looked helplessly to Daniel who searched the young man's face with pleading eyes for him to accept Beatrice and comfort her as only he could.

Jeremiah stepped closer, "'Tis all right, Mother... we're all together, now." Daniel stepped to the side and Jeremiah put his arms awkwardly around her, and the two wept tears for the lost years.

Relieved, Daniel watched gratefully while Jeremiah withdrew his handkerchief. "Now, wipe away the tears, we must hurry, 'tis time to celebrate. May I be takin' the honor, Mr. O'Leardon?"

"Certainly, lad," Daniel beamed.

Joseph began playing, once the doors closed and Jeremiah walked down the aisle with Beatrice, presenting her to the curious guests. Hushed whispers streamed through the pews, questioning the identity of the attractive woman on his arm. Her striking resemblance to the bride was unexpected, to say the least. Beatrice sat down next to her son, Henry, gently squeezing the hand of each of the family members and kissing the foreheads of her two grandsons, Marvin and Conrad.

At this point, Albert Zigmann was, by far, the most delighted to see Daniel take his place next to the mysterious woman in the first pew. Any pangs of resentment and jealousy toward the overly accommodating bookstore owner, Daniel, were immediately extinguished.

Outside the church, Rahzvon quickly unloaded his troupe to the front door and then drove around back to hitch Duff to the wedding carriage. He parked it out front and looked over his masterpiece.

"Stand proud, Duff! I am sorry, but it had to be done. A great responsibility has been bestowed upon you," he said in jest, rubbing the horse's muzzle. He looked up to see Joseph's disturbed gaze, eying the strange animal.

Rahzvon ignored it, straightened his tie, and brushed off his boots with disgust. *I need my own clothing. I need my inheritance.*

Joseph's piping greeted Rahzvon at the double doors. Rahzvon entered the beautifully decorated room and spotted Sophia and the Wheaton girls with the help of Jeanie's waving arms to lure him her way. Rahzvon moved swiftly down the aisle, until the new faces next to Daniel, in the first pew, distracted him. His gaze immediately refocused on the pew accommodated by the girls and Sophia—more specifically, the *party* next to Sophia. Rahzvon locked glares with the seafaring phantom rival, Mr. Henry McTavish. Rahzvon took his place next to Jeanie, who, on the other hand, could not be more pleased with the wide gap between her hero and Sophia. He gave Jeanie a brief smile and then casually glanced at Sophia, now engaged in a seemingly pleasant conversation with Tavy, the over-confident sailor. Rahzvon's muscles tensed, his jaw went taut. He turned slowly to face the pulpit.

The church doors opened for the final time before the ceremony. The last guest entered and Joseph stopped playing the bagpipes and followed, closing the doors behind him. The congregation turned as the smartly dressed stranger moved smoothly down the aisle and took the empty place next to Rahzvon. Rahzvon, preoccupied with Sophia's diversion, turned in surprise to find the beautiful young woman seated next to him.

"*Hello*," Rahzvon greeted.

"Good afternoon," the woman replied.

Rahzvon then made a slow calculated turn toward Sophia and displayed a wide satisfied grin. Sophia's creased brow and narrowed eyes assured him that justice had been served. Rahzvon leaned back, content and relaxed, folding his arms across his chest.

Joseph began playing again when the ceremony began and Hiram solemnly entered the front of the church. The best man made a brief double take of Daniel's guest. Her resemblance to Naomi sent a cold shiver through Hiram's body. In receiving Daniel's nod of confirmation, Hiram's heart warmed with the prospects of Naomi and Edward's delight. His broad dimpled smile stirred the entire audience, for the Master of McDonnally Manor rarely displayed emotion in public. Beatrice observed the new arrival in awe. *Miss Nettlepin was not exaggerating,* she thought.

As for the schoolteacher, her heart raced the moment Hiram appeared and she began fanning her face with her handkerchief. Likewise, the other single women sighed in concert. The married males in the audience shifted uneasily as they observed the interested eyes of their wives, but made every effort to show no sign of their displeasure.

Edward followed shortly. His weak legs struggled to maintain a smooth stride to the altar. With a glimpse of the front pew, he stopped and his eyes widened. Daniel, seeing Edward's expected reaction, immediately left his seat and whispered to the shocked groom.

"Yer surprise for Naomi. Good work, man!"

Edward stood staring at Beatrice, marveling at the similarity to his bride. The crowd was silent. Edward walked slowly over to Beatrice and reached for her hand. He kissed it lovingly. Anticipating Naomi's reaction, feeling sheer euphoria, he smiled and resumed his place before the altar. The audience, too, now waited with baited breath to see the bride's response.

The heartfelt piping continued as Allison entered as Chief Bridesmaid. A moment later her steps slowed with confusion in seeing the woman who she knew could be none other than her long-lost grandmother. Tears appeared on Allison's cheeks with each step closer to the strangely familiar, yet older face.

"Grandmother?" she asked nervously.

"Yes, Allison," Beatrice replied.

They wept until Beatrice hastened her from the touching scene, back to her position.

With the playing of the bride's introduction, everyone in the room rose, nervously anticipating Naomi's reaction to the mystery guest. Naomi entered slowly, stepping in time to the music. Behind the lace veil, she focused on Edward's endearing smile. He waited for just the right moment when she stopped next to him, to direct her gaze to the first pew with a guiding glance. Jeremiah's shy grin greeted Naomi. Her eyes moved quickly to the young man sitting next to him.

The young man from the shop? Her thoughts raced. *Could it be?* She glanced to the young woman next to him, then the two little smiling faces and then...

Mama? She let go of her bouquet with one hand and grasped Edward's arm to steady herself.

Joseph stopped playing and the guests watched with concern. Overcome with dread of rejection and ruination of her daughter's wedding, Beatrice's hands began to tremble. Daniel tightened his grasp on her hand. Edward put his arm around Naomi and escorted her to the pew.

Beatrice mouthed her daughter's name, but could not speak.

"Mama!" Naomi wailed.

A second later, the two women were embraced, sobbing uncontrollably. Nearly every man and woman in the church withdrew their handkerchiefs and shared in their joy. When Naomi regained her ability to speak, she whispered to Beatrice.

"I prayed every night for this day, Mama."

"I too, my dear daughter."

They took turns wiping each other's tears.

"Edward, Allison, this is Mama, I mean my mother," she gave a little laugh.

"Yes, love." Edward hugged Allison.

"And this, Naomi," Beatrice touched Henry's hand, "is your brother, Henry. I do believe that you have met."

"Yes, yes we have," Naomi agreed, sniffling.

Naomi hugged Henry and ran her fingers through his auburn waves, identical to Jeremiah's.

Naomi then moved to embrace Jeremiah and kissed his cheek.

Naomi then reached for Pearl's hand, "Hello, I am Naomi."

"Hello, I am Pearl and these two fine lads are your nephews, Marvin and Conrad."

"My pleasure, Marvin, Conrad. I am your Aunt Naomi. Look, Edward, at all the kin I have!" Naomi exclaimed.

"Yes, love. Do you think that we might take a minute now, so that I may become one of them?" he teased.

"Oh, my, yes!" Naomi gave Beatrice one last kiss and wiped her tears.

Hiram watched silently at the altar. He revisited the years that he had spent comforting Naomi in their youth, ironically, those times when she felt the loss of her mother. Despite his involvement with Abigail, Hiram felt the ingrained nagging guilt of neglecting his duty to comfort and protect Naomi. But, he stood tall, concealing his emotions and watching Edward console her.

The bride and groom resumed their positions at the altar and the clergyman motioned for the guests to take their seats.

Sophia watched the scene, now growing anxious to see *her* mother, Hannah, Hiram's twin. *Mama, you shall be at my wedding to Rahzvon, if I have to go all the way to Paris to fetch you.*

Tavy's large hand fell across Harriet Dugan's stout little fingers and gave them a grateful squeeze in appreciation for her role as his surrogate mother. Dagmar, Naomi's stepmother, felt a sense of relief with the reunion of Naomi and her mother, compensating for the ill deeds of her estranged husband.

During the ceremony, another mother was rushing to her husband's bedside. Maryanne Wheaton had received word that her husband, Bruce, had regained consciousness. She left Dara, the second youngest daughter, with Mrs. Stewart, who would not be attending the wedding, along with a note for Harriet Dugan to look after the children. Maryanne took the infant, Martha, with her. Maryanne's decision to miss the McDonnally wedding was unfortunate, but necessary.

A loud crashing of thunder startled the guests and all but two, quickly redirected their attention to the service. Sophia and Rahzvon's thoughts clashed with alarming expressions midway across the pew.

Duff!

The aftereffects of a downpour would prove to be disastrous for the poor "grey horse" of good fortune. Sophia and Rahzvon slid uncomfortably back in the pew while the spring rain pummeled the church windows.

Before the bride and groom took their vows and knelt in prayer, Hiram bound their hands with the tartan cloth. Hiram looked down at Naomi. Subconsciously introducing him, Naomi smiled at Hiram, then to her mother. Suddenly, Naomi realized she had not acknowledged his presence with the earlier introductions to her family. Her smile melted, sorry that she had slighted him. A fleeting moment of unspoken words passed between them—one last second of their past to be swept away forever when Edward placed the gold band engraved with the Celtic knots on her finger.

At the end of the ceremony, Hiram nervously placed a sash of the McDonnally tartan on Naomi and pinned it with the clan badge. His proud smile barely surfaced. A hundred thoughts crossed through Naomi's memories as she felt lost in the intense eyes of Hiram Geoffrey McDonnally, but only one prevailed. She turned to Edward, her heart gladdened to, once again, accept the name of Mrs. Edward McDonnally.

"It is official, Naomi. You truly are a McDonnally," Hiram announced.

"Yes, I *am*," she took Edward's arm and they walked to the call of Joseph's bagpipes toward the back of the church.

The rain had ceased and the elated crowd gathered around the wedding carriage, prepared to greet the bride and groom with the tossing of petals. Edward threw silver coins for the children, who scrambled for the treasure, but the floral shower ceased when Naomi and Edward paused before the carriage and stared with curiosity. The cheers from the crowd quickly subsided as all joined in their observation of the dark zebra-like creature standing in dark puddles covering the white stones.

"Duff?" Edward asked.

The ridiculous condition of the innocent beast spurred a great humorous response from the onlookers. Amidst the laughter, Rahzvon immediately sought the hand of his accomplice and the guilty couple casually slipped to safety in the depth of the preoccupied crowd. This move dually satisfied Rahzvon's discomforting situations; it not only removed them from the scrutiny of the wedding party, but distanced Sophia from the overly attentive sailor.

The bride and groom shrugged off the confusion of the horse. In a flurry of flying petals, they drove away from the church to the reception at their home.

Chapter IX

"The Reception"

"Of all the torments, all the cares,
With which our lives are curst;
Of all the plagues a lover bears,
Sure rivals are the worst!"

—William Walsh

Edward opened the door to Brachney Hall and positioned himself to carry his bride over the threshold.

"Are you quite sure that you can do this?" Naomi asked with concern.

"No, but I shall die trying. Prepare yourself."

Naomi held her breath trying to lighten his load. Edward slowly lifted her, straining his weakened arm and leg. He quickly shifted her to an awkward but viable angle to his good side and with knees bent took two steps to victory.

"I did it!" Edward shouted, after lowering Naomi to the floor.

Sophia called from behind. "Yes, of course, you did! You are the Great Uncle Edward!" Her cheer led the crew of on-looking guests in a round of applause. Edward blushing, faced his audience, bowed at the waist, and hastened Naomi upstairs to prepare for the guests.

At the entrance to the ballroom, Edward reached up to the tartans and tied the MacKenzie and McDonnally plaids in the knot to begin the festivities. The bride and groom moved inside to form the traditional reception line with their relatives. Feeling extremely guilty for her neglect, Naomi immediately, led her mother over to Hiram.

"Mother, this is Hiram McDonnally, Edward's nephew, he—" Naomi began when her mother interrupted.

"Naomi, we have met. Daniel introduced us at the church after the ceremony." She threw Hiram a smile of approval.

Naomi looked nervously toward Hiram, as well, and only half-smiled. "Very well then, I suppose we should get in line." All went smoothly until another unexpected moment when Naomi introduced her brother to the Dugan party.

"Henry, Pearl, these are our dear friends the Dugans. This is Harriet and Joseph. This handsome young man is Tavy, rather, Henry McTa—oh, dear, Naomi laughed, "we have another *Henry*. This day is full of surprises. Henry, may I introduce, Henry McTavish, their *son*."

The two smiling men shook hands.

"Grand name, *Henry*," Naomi's brother commented.

"None finer," Tavy agreed.

Trina Dunmore listened to the interesting exchange while she waited in line behind the Dugan family.

While the introductions continued, Rahzvon was busy deterring Sophia on the staircase in hopes of stealing a kiss from the woman he considered to be the loveliest in the village. With each step forward, Rahzvon blocked Sophia's advancement.

"Sir, have you lost your sense of direction to the ballroom?"

"I have not."

"Am I to understand that there is purpose to my deterrence?"

"The first dance is mine."

"Very, well." She started to move forward, but Rahzvon remained steadfast.

"The second dance is mine," Rahzvon insisted.

Sophia looked at him skeptically. "Yes, you may have the second dance."

Before she had a chance to raise her foot, Rahzvon announced, "All the dances are mine... except one, no two."

"Am I to understand that you have granted me permission to dance two dances with the men of my choice?" She smiled coyly, "Perhaps, even with..."

"One with the groom and one with your uncle, Hiram," Rahzvon designated.

"Should I thank you for your gallant generosity, sir?" she said sarcastically.

"Proper etiquette would demand it."

"Very well, I thank you kind sir," she said humbly and curtseyed.

"I apologize, but I did not hear what you said. Remember, men have difficulty hearing. Come closer." He reached for her waist and pulled her in. His lips touched hers when a shout behind them interrupted.

"There ya be, Miss Muffet!"

"Tavy," Sophia responded.

"I found 'em!"

"You did?" Sophia replied excitedly. "Where?"

"In the wooden crate in the scullery!"

"Delightful!"

During this unsavory exchange, Rahzvon released his grip about Sophia and stood with his brows knitted with reproach.

"I shall be meetin' wit' ya later, to *show* ya," Tavy promised. He then reached out to touch Sophia's hand. Rahzvon straightened objectionably with their contact.

"Ye be savin' me a dance, Miss Muffet," Henry said in a hushed tone, turned and grinned at Rahzvon.

Henry McTavish blew in with the power of the storming sea winds and left behind considerable damage.

Sophia stood smiling with satisfaction to the sailor's report while Rahzvon stared at her with censure.

"*Miss Muffet?*" he asked sternly.

"Yes, Miss Muffet," she answered, still reeling with the joy of Henry's find.

"Why?" he demanded.

"Why what, Rahzvon?"

"Why the name?"

"Miss Muffet? It was Tavy's idea after an incident at the Dugan shed," Sophia answered without concern,

Razvon's eyes narrowed with negativity. "At the *Dugan shed?*"

"Oh yes," Sophia giggled remembering the scene. "We were talking in the Dugan shed, Tavy and I, when this horrid spider sat down beside me, like in the nursery rhyme and frightened me so badly that I flew into his arms and..."

Sophia stopped in seeing Rahzvon's escalating disapproval. He moved up one step away from her.

"Rahzvon, we were only *talking*...he has some French books that were his fa— "

Before she had a chance to finish, Rahzvon turned and headed for the ballroom. Sophia panicked and followed him, only to be intercepted by her uncle Hiram in the doorway.

"In a hurry, Sophia?"

"Yes," she answered with distraction.

"It is a little late, my dear. The reception line has dispensed. *Where* have you been, lassie? You were supposed to be standing in line next to me?" he reprimanded.

Sophia looked up at him with astonishment.

"Uncle Hiram, I am so very sorry. I lost track of time."

"Save your apologies for your Uncle Edward and your Aunt Naomi," he said coldly and left to speak with the orchestra.

Naomi and Edward joined hands and walked to the center of the floor to dance their first dance as Mr. and Mrs. Edward McDonnally. Everyone in the room could feel the extraordinary significance of this special moment. It was held with nearly as high regard as the one in which they were declared man and wife, an hour earlier.

Hiram watched, towering over Abigail who was tucked under his arm. Albert reached down and clasped Eloise's hand, while Daniel looked to Beatrice with great appreciation. However, Allison was snubbing Guillaume, and steaming over the presence of his ex-fiancé, Trina.

Sophia arrived in the nick of time to snatch the hands of Conrad and Marvin, who were determined to join the bride and groom, while Rahzvon assessed the area in search for his insolent rival. When the guests scattered throughout the ballroom, Guillaume spotted Rahzvon looking very disturbed and approaching Tavy from behind. Guillaume moved quickly to detain him, suspecting that Rahzvon was about to offer his objections to his unscrupulous designs on Sophia. Guillaume grabbed his arm.

"No, man, I have a better idea," Guillaume whispered.

Rahzvon fought his retaliatory instincts and followed Guillaume to the opposite side of the room. Rahzvon was breathing hard, his good sense being eaten away with resentment.

"Rahzvon, listen to me. Forget about McTavish for a minute. I have a plan."

Rahzvon tried to restrain his antagonism while Guillaume explained.

"Old man, you are not the only one with *woman* difficulties."

"I have no difficulties with women, I am going to take him apart!" Rahzvon lunged forward when Guillaume caught his sleeve and moved directly in front of him."

"Think, man, think! This is a wedding—Sophie's aunt and uncle's. If you cause a disturbance, Sophie shall never forgive you and Hiram shall put you out of your misery."

Rahzvon took a breath and loosened his collar. "*Miss Muffet.*" He snarled.

"*Miss Muffet?*" Guillaume looked confused then continued, "Now, I was saying, Allison is a fit to be tied with Trina's arrival. You can imagine, you know *Allison.* I *told* her that I never invited Trina to Lochmoor. Whether or not she believes me is another matter."

"How does this concern me?" Rahzvon asked, looking annoyed in McTavish's direction.

"McTavish concerns you," Guillaume pointed out.

"Yeah?"

"McTavish is the solution to both our problems."

"Are you daft, Zigmann?"

"No, McTavish fancies himself to be a lady's man. He has come to the reception alone. Trina is here *alone.* They are perfectly suited for one another."

"Are you as blind as you are bonkers?"

"Look at Trina, Rahzvon. She is frightfully sophisticated and he is a common sailor. It is positively, perfect!"

"As usual, your logic escapes me."

"There is no need for unnecessary criticism. It is a basic mathematical equation: one lonely attractive woman, one rugged sailor. Opposites attract, as they say."

Rahzvon shook his head. "It shall never work, Zigmann. I am getting something to drink."

Guillaume frowned with disappointment as Rahzvon left.

You may not appreciate my intellectual genius right now, but you soon shall.

While the adults mingled and danced, the youngest generation amused themselves. Little Jeanie Wheaton spent much of her time following her hero, Rahzvon, throughout the crowd. She never gave notice that she, too, was being pursued. Henry and Pearl's youngest son, Marvin, found Jeanie Wheaton to be fascinating. He watched her every move from a safe distance.

When Rahzvon approached Sophia, Jeanie retreated off to the side like your typical wallflower, alone and bored. Young Marvin took this opportunity to make himself known. He stood posted next to her, innocuously watching the dance partners whirling across the floor. He inched his way closer to the little girl, a head shorter.

"Miss, would you care to see something grand?"

Jeanie shyly shrugged.

Rahzvon saw Sophia standing at the refreshment table. He ran his fingers back through his hair and went over to speak with her. *You look entirely too irresistible for me to leave you to his advances,* he thought.

"I missed the first dance. Would you please do me the honor of joining me for this one, Miss McDonnally?"

Sophia looked at Rahzvon curiously.

I would like to dance with you, I have never had the pleasure.

Sophia nodded and took his arm.

Once they were moving smoothly across the floor, Sophia immediately realized the expertise of her partner's abilities. *I should not be surprised—you were groomed in the royal court,* she thought.

Sophia noticed Jeanie's suitor and commented, "It appears that young Marvin may have stolen your girl."

Rahzvon turned to see Jeanie laughing with the little boy balancing a cup of punch on his head.

"His talents are greater than mine," Rahzvon laughed.

"Are you not feeling betrayed in seeing your little admirer so easily diverted?"

"Not in the least. She is the *one* young lady that I do not mind losing to another's attention," Rahzvon said sternly, as he spun Sophia around.

Since the dance began, Guillaume had procured notepaper from the desk, in the hall outside the ballroom, and the pen from the small table displaying the guest book. He composed two notes, folded them, and addressed one to his ex-fiancé, Trina, the other to Rahzvon's menacing sailor, Henry McTavish.

Guillaume placed the papers in his jacket pocket and began searching the crowd for the perfect candidate to deliver the messages. Every face which he encountered presented a new set of problems in his choice. Alas, he found someone who could be trusted, someone who could be bribed. *But can he read?* Guillaume questioned. *Surely, he can.* Guillaume studied the little boy's face and height. *He must be six or seven.* Guillaume moved through the crowd to Henry and Pearl's son, Conrad. Conrad was playing quietly with Naomi's kitten.

"Hello, that is a cute kitten you have there," Guillaume remarked.

"It is not mine; it belongs to my Aunt Naomi."

Guillaume leaned over to pet the kitten.

"Young man, could I persuade you to perform a small task for me, to deliver a couple of notes...to people here in the ballroom?"

"Shall you pay me?" Conrad shot back.

"Pay you? Money?" Guillaume asked disapprovingly.

"No, sir, I suppose not. But I shall, if you fetch me a drink and hold the kitten until I return," Conrad said keenly.

"Do you know how to read?"

"Yes, I can read," Conrad snapped.

"Very well, do you know the guests by name?"

"Most of them," Conrad looked through the crowd.

Guillaume led Conrad closer to get a better view of Trina.

"Do you see that lovely woman over there, talking with Mr. McDonnally?"

"Mrs. Dugan?" Conrad asked.

"No, that is Edward McDonnally. I am referring to the woman speaking with his nephew,

Hiram McDonnally. See the tall man over there." Guillaume motioned as discreetly as possible.

"He is frightfully tall to be a nephew."

"Never mind that. The woman with whom he is speaking, is Trina. Now, where is he? There, look over there," Guillaume motioned.

Conrad moved closer to Guillaume.

"That rough looking character is a sailor, named McTavish."

"A *real* sailor?" Conrad asked, amazed.

"Yes, a real sailor."

"Does he have a tattoo?"

"I have no idea! Now, here take these. Give me the kitten." Guillaume took the kitten and handed Conrad the notes. "Conrad, this is a surprise, so do not reveal the fact that I gave you these and deliver them with as much secrecy as possible. Do you understand?"

"I am not an infant," Conrad said indignantly.

"Very well, go to it. I shall have your refreshment waiting for you."

Guillaume pulled the kitten from his shoulder and went to the refreshment table.

Conrad read the names on the notes and set out to deliver them.

"*Adieu* to evening dances,
when merry neighbors meet,
and the fiddle says to boys and girls,
get up and shake your feet!"

—William Allingham

Chapter X

"Confetti"

"Heat not a furnace
For your foe so hot
That it do singe yourself."

—William Shakespeare

Conrad went over to the *tall nephew* and found him speaking with his newly acquired uncle, Jeremiah. The woman was gone. Conrad continued his search for Trina. After checking every corner, he finally discovered her by the veranda. He approached her cautiously, checking every direction for prying eyes. He handed Trina the note with inscribed with her name.

"Thank you, sir." Trina looked at the folded paper with wonder as the little messenger vanished in the crowd.Trina opened the note and read it.

Miss Trina,
With you being the most handsome woman in the room, I found myself compelled to ask you to share a few minutes alone with me, so that I might introduce myself.

Trina stopped reading, disturbed that such a young boy would write "such" a note. She continued.

My shyness prevents me from approaching you publicly. Please meet me in the garden at 5:30.
Tavy, the sailor

Oh, it is not from him. Tavy, the sailor*? Strange man.*

She looked around the room and saw him speaking with Hiram.

What a man! It was such a pleasure speaking with him. The sailor is not too awfully plain, either— a little rough around the edges, but handsome in a rustic sense. A son of the Dugan's? she remembered from the reception line. *I see no harm in a brief meeting with him. No harm at all. Besides, Guillaume is ignoring me.*

She folded the note and placed it in her pocketbook. She pulled out the tiny gold timepiece. *I have not long to wait.*

Conrad stopped near the table with the guestbook and read the name on the remaining note.

"Why it says *Henry.* It is for Father! This *is* a surprise." Conrad set out to find his father.

Guillaume balanced the kitten on his shoulder with one hand and filled the cup with the other. He scanned the room and spotted McTavish, but saw no sign of Conrad and assumed that the mission was accomplished.

Conrad darted past the Stewarts talking to his grandmother and found his father talking to a man who the little boy believed to be the postman. *Today, I am the postman,* Conrad thought proudly. He crept behind his father where he dropped the note into Henry's pocket and shot behind a potted plant. His father noted the disturbance and reached into his pocket after Mr. Kilvert excused himself. He removed the folded paper addressed to simply, *Henry.* He opened it and read it.

> *Henry,*
> *I am knew to Lochmoor, unknown to most of the guests.*

Henry paused. *Knew?*
He continued reading.

> *When I first saw you in the church, I found myself quite taken with you. I would like to become better acquainted. Meet me in the garden at 5:30.*
> *Trina Dunmore*

Poor girl, she cannot spell, was Henry's initial reaction then, *Poor girl! She must know that I am married... meet her at a half past five!*

Henry fumbled with the note, and stuffed it into his pocket. He glanced nervously around, and then pulled out his pocket watch, noting that it was nearly five-thirty. He looked up and there *she* was only a few yards away. He stared blankly at the author of the cryptic note. Trina noticed Henry's attentiveness and smiled unconcerned in his direction.

Trina's smile sent Henry in search of his wife's protective wing. He found her laughing with Harriet, Eloise and Dagmar.

"Excuse me, Pearl; would you care to take a stroll with me?" Henry asked in desperation.

"Not now, Henry, I am speaking with these ladies about our cat, Fritzie." Pearl turned away from her husband and continued her conversation about the clever feline.

Henry moved slowly through the room. His eyes darted from face to face. The young woman was gone. He checked his watch. *She has gone to meet me in the garden!* he panicked. *I shan't go! What if she persists? What if she tries to contact me? What if Pearl discovers Trina's infatuation with me?* He looked over in his wife's direction. *No, no I have to nip this in the bud. I had better go.*

In his attempt to leave the ballroom, he saw Trina tying one of the Wheaton girl's hair ribbons.

Good, I found her before she left. I need to speak with her here. It would do me no good to be found with her in the garden.

He looked over the room and spotted an empty table near the wall. *Better yet, the veranda—no one is out there.*

Slowly, Henry gathered his courage to address his admirer. With sweating palms and a racing heart, he forced himself toward the unknown.

He spoke with great difficulty, "Miss Dunmore?"

"Yes?" Trina looked at the obviously distraught man, a few years her senior.

"May, may I speak with you on the veranda for only, only a minute?"

"Well, I..." Trina baulked, knowing that she should be leaving to meet with Tavy in the garden.

"I know that you expected to meet in the garden, but..." Henry stumbled.

Trina looked confused with his knowledge of her scheduled meeting with the sailor.

"Very well," she hesitated and then followed him to the veranda.

On the other side of the ballroom, Guillaume finally located Conrad playing with Jeanie and Marvin.

"Conrad, I have been looking for you. Here is your drink and the cat."

"I already had a drink." The little boy ignored Guillaume and continued his game with the children.

Guillaume looked over at McTavish, who should have been heading to the garden by now. *Fool! Turning down one of the most beaut—Trina.* Guillaume sipped the drink and fought to keep the kitten from climbing on his head. *Is he so taken with Sophia that he would not take the opportunity to meet with Trina? No, not Tavy.*

Guillaume turned to Conrad.

"Conrad, come here."

"What now, sir? More notes to deliver?"

"Shh! Did you deliver both notes?"

"Yes, I delivered them," Conrad said proudly. "One to the woman and the other to my father. He did not even know that it was me delivering it—I hid like a spy." Conrad ran back to his friends.

Guillaume stood dumbfounded. *His father? Why would Conrad give it to his father, Henry? Henry, oh, no, why do these things happen to me?*

Juggling the small kitten and the empty cup, Guillaume shot past the guests. Allison rolled her eyes as he passed. He ran over to Rahzvon and Sophia.

"What is it man?" Rahzvon asked.

"You have to help me—something frightful has happened! I have made a terrible mistake!"

Sophia shook her head. "Oh no, I am not going to be a party to this, whatever it is." Sophia left without hesitation to dance with her Uncle Hiram in hopes of getting back in his good graces.

Rahzvon pulled Guillaume to the corner.

"What have you done, Zigmann?"

"My scheme has gone awry!"

"What scheme?"

"To get Trina and McTavish together. Now Trina is with the wrong Henry!"

"Zigmann, calm down and explain and take that cat off of your head."

Guillaume handed the cat to Rahzvon who placed it gently on the floor. Guillaume rubbed his forehead with distress.

"I wrote two notes, one for Trina from Tavy, the other from Tavy to Trina, each relaying their interest in the other and desire to meet in the garden at half past five."

"*Zigmann...*" Rahzvon reprimanded.

"I convinced Naomi's nephew to deliver them. I addressed the one for McTavish, with *Henry*. It sounded more formal. But the lad got confused and thought it was for his *father*."

"Are you mad? He is a married man! He thinks that *Trina* wrote this note?"

"Yes." Guillaume said with despair.

"And Trina believes that Naomi's *brother* wrote her the note?"

"No. I signed it, *Tavy*."

"Do you realize that you have possibly destroyed the lives of two innocent people?" Rahzvon threatened.

"Yes. What am I to do?" Guillaume panicked.

"Go to the garden and explain, now!"

"What shall they think of me?"

"Swallow your pride and get down there, man," Rahzvon demanded. Guillaume left for the garden without another thought.

Several minutes later, Rahzvon was reviewing the disaster when he spotted Trina and Henry on the veranda. A shockwave ran through his body. *She is supposed to be talking with Guillaume in the garden. What is Henry saying to her? She has no idea what he is talking about; she never wrote that note. I have to stop this.* Rahzvon moved toward the veranda. There, Henry continued to explain to Trina.

"Miss, I am a married man. I have children."

"Yes, I know, I met them," Trina smiled.

Is she so drawn to me that she has no consideration for my children, my life with my family? Henry fretted.

Trina interrupted Henry, "Excuse me, sir, but it is getting late."

"Miss, the garden is a mistake!"

At that moment, Rahzvon arrived and took Trina by the arm.

"Excuse us, Henry; I need to speak with Miss Dunmore for a minute." Rahzvon began pulling her away.

"We shall talk later!" Trina called out.

Henry closed his eyes in dread of Trina's promise.

Rahzvon pulled Trina to the vacant table. "Please have a seat."

"Sir, I am flattered. I enjoyed sitting next to you at the wedding, but I have a previous engagement," Trina insisted.

"No, no you do not," Rahzvon said shaking his head.

"I beg your pardon?"

"Miss, it is a mistake."

"Have all the men in Lochmoor gone mad?"

"Miss, you did receive a note from Mr. McTavish, did you not?"

"This is none of your concern! I am appalled," Trina started to leave.

Sophia, now standing a few feet away with Harriet Dugan witnessed the confrontation.

"I am telling you, it was a mistake," Rahzvon repeated.

Harriet Dugan cast a suspicious eye, "What do ya suppose is troublin' those two?" she asked Sophia.

"I do not know, but I am about to find out," Sophia steamed.

"Sir, I am quite capable of making my own decisions," Trina scorned.

"Rahzvon, what goes on here?" Sophia demanded.

Sophia was the last person who he desired to see at that moment.

"If this man is a friend of yours, you should inform him of the necessity of formal introduction!" Trina scorned.

"We met at the church; you sat right next to me," Rahzvon retaliated, raising his voice.

Trina ignored his comment and addressed Sophia. "He shall never earn the affections of any decent woman with these methods!"

Trina stormed off to the garden.

Sophia's dark eyes raged with fury and her body stiffened. Rahzvon took her by the shoulders and guided her to the veranda like a little cannon. Henry was still standing there, contemplating his next plan of action to rid himself of the love-struck beauty.

"Excuse us, Henry, might we have the privacy of the veranda?" Rahzvon asked.

"I need to find my wife," is all that Henry said before he left.

Rahzvon closed the veranda doors behind Sophia, frozen in statue form.

"Phia, trust me. Guillaume is responsible for this."

Sophia's face began to distort with jealous rage. Rahzvon saw no alternative. He had to act quickly. He grabbed her and kissed her like no other kiss they had shared.

Sophia's hand sprung back to slap him when Rahzvon intercepted hers with his and demanded, "You shall listen."

Rahzvon began explaining Guillaume's scheme and Henry's involvement. Sophia listened, gradually realizing Rahzvon's innocence in the matter.

"Poor Henry...*Naomi's brother*. Since Naomi is my great aunt and he is her brother, is he my uncle—" Sophia began pensively.

"No, Phia," Rahzvon cut her off.

"That Guillaume Zigmann—Uncle was right, trouble follows him. I have always considered him a dear friend, but this is the last straw. I am going to have a discussion with him that he shall not soon forget!" She reached for the door handle.

"Halt, m' lady." Rahzvon blocked the doorway. "I shall deal with Zigmann. You are not to get involved. Trina has gone to the garden and she shall meet Guillaume there. He is going to explain and *if* he survives her wrath, he shall have to inform Naomi's brother of his part in that ridiculous plan. Now, *you* owe me a dance."

Sophia followed him to the center of the dance floor without another word. She had suffered from enough excitement that day. Harriet watched the two emerge from the veranda. Any gossip of Rahzvon and Sophia's parting quickly dissolved with their amiable reunion on the dance floor.

Guillaume, now feeling totally humiliated by his immaturity, paced nervously in the garden. Trina arrived, surprised to find her former fiancé and no sign of the enamored sailor.

"Guillaume?"

"Hello, Trina."

She looked around and then asked. "Have you seen, Tavy... the uh...sailor?"

Tavy, the sailor. The words burned in his skull as scorching proof that Trina had read the note.

"He is not coming, Trina."

"What *ever* are you talking about?"

"McTavish is not meeting you here. He was to meet you at a half past five. It was a mistake."

A mistake? she thought. The haunting repetition of the words she had heard from several men, finally made sense.

"Is this the way that beastly sailor takes charge of his affairs?" she shouted. "He invites a woman, then changes his mind and sends his lackeys to do his bidding? I have never been so insulted! I am going to give that arrogant, inconsiderate, coward a piece of my mind!"

Trina took off running toward Brachney Hall.

"Wait Trina, you are mistaken!" Guillaume called after her. In his pursuit up the stairs, Guillaume met Naomi's brother, Henry, recovering from a near heart attack when Trina came running toward him.

"Mr. Zigmann, might I have a word with you?"

Guillaume looked frantically toward the stairs, "Can it wait?"

"No, it is of the utmost importance. I need to confide in you as a peer and someone outside of the McDonnally clan," Henry explained.

Guillaume, knowingly, sat down on the stairs to face his deserved fate.

Trina whipped past the couples gathered in the ballroom, combing for the doomed sailor. Once she spotted her target, she made a beeline for him, grabbed his hand and began dragging him toward the hall. Tavy smiled with delight as the young beauty pulled him past the interested spectators.

"Oh, oh, she has got him," Rahzvon noted catching a glimpse of the departing couple.

"Come with me, Sophia." Rahzvon rushed after them, pulling Sophia with him.

Trina marched on out of the ballroom to the north end of the hall and halted next to the writing desk where the chaos originated. She flung Tavy's arm loose with disgust.

"And who might ya be, feisty lassie?" he asked.

"*Who* might I be? Very amusing! This game may be successful with the riff raff in your social circles, but in high society, it is considered to be crude, outlandish and positively unacceptable!"

Trina raised her hand to him, when Sophia called out, "No Trina, he is innocent!"

"Miss Muffet, come to me rescue?" Tavy called back.

Rahzvon immediately lost all desire to help the cocky sailor, but Sophia proceeded to explain the mix-up. Guillaume and Henry arrived shortly thereafter where Guillaume humbly received the daggering stares of his disgruntled peers.

"My apologies to each and every one of you; it was a foolish idea. I never meant for anyone to suffer discomfort. I explained the situation to Henry—this Henry."

They looked at Guillaume with warranted skepticism.

"Accurately, I might add!" Guillaume defended.

No one responded.

"Look at me; I stand here, bare before you, stripped of my pride. Say whatever you desire, I deserve a thousand tongue-lashings. McTavish, Trina, I merely thought that the two of you would get along famously," Guillaume explained.

Tavy looked over at Trina. Trina looked uncomfortably away, then back in reconsideration.

"Mr. McTavish, I am Trina Dunmore. I, too, offer my apologies. I had no right to embarrass you in front of your friends and family with my assumptions. In doing so, I share your embarrassment."

Tavy grinned at Trina. "Lassie, ye may drag me all o'er Scotland, any time ye hae a mind to." Trina looked nervously away; Tavy gave an unconcerned shrug and smiled again at Sophia.

Rahzvon stepped possessively closer to her.

"Please, say something, someone," Guillaume pleaded.

Sophia and Trina, aware of Guillaume's faults and frailties, felt tinges of sympathy for him, while Rahzvon, who held honor in the highest regard, found Guillaume's confession admirable, although undoubtedly, inevitable. Naomi's brother, Henry, was thankful that he was married and no longer involved in this romantic intrigue and Tavy was simply amused by the fact that any man would go to such lengths to distance himself from such a beautiful woman. Guillaume offered one last plea.

"I realize that I am not deserving of any favors from any one of you, but could you, please, withhold information of this incident from Allison?"

The five shared conferring grins as Henry reached in his jacket and removed the crumpled note and Trina opened her pocketbook to surrender the evidence.

Guillaume was staring at the relinquished pieces of paper with eternal gratitude when Allison spoke behind him.

"Guillaume, has the reception moved to the hall?"

Guillaume turned and began tearing the notes into tiny pieces that fell to the floor.

"Confetti, we were discussing confetti to celebrate this unforgettable day."

Chapter XI

"Surprise Gift"

"For when of pleasure she doth sing,
My thoughts enjoy a sudden spring;
But if she doth of sorrow speak,
Even from my heart the strings do break."

—Thomas Campion

Once the bride and groom cut the tiered cake and shared that first piece, Abigail left Hiram to become better acquainted with Pearl and Edward became absorbed in a conversation with Jeremiah about his new motorcar. Naomi wandered over to get another beverage when she met Hiram at the refreshment table.

"Naomi, my apologies for my niece's absence from the reception line," Hiram offered while filling her cup.

"I am certain that Sophia had a good reason."

"That 'good reason' sleeps in my barn and it does not have four legs."

Naomi giggled. "Did Sophia tell you that she found the wedding band at my party last night?"

"Aye, she made it very clear that she shall be the next to be married," Hiram said with despair.

"Hiram she *is* nearly twenty."

"When I was twenty, I—" Hiram stopped short. Naomi looked away uncomfortably.

Hiram began again, "Shall we discuss something less disconcerting?"

Naomi looked at him without a suggestion. Hiram, too, found himself at a loss of words. Mention of the past was more disruptive than either expected. Naomi sipped her drink. As her conscience demanded, she finally spoke.

"Hiram, I feel very distressed over the fact that I neglected to introduce you to my family at the church. Please accept my deepest apology," Naomi lowered her head.

"Aye, Naomi, I have been meaning to discuss that with you," Hiram said ominously.

"You have?" Naomi mumbled, looking up at him.

"Perhaps, one could excuse one's oversight if one had something...something important pre-occupying one's thoughts but..." Hiram gently reprimanded with a tone of disappointment.

Guilt-ridden, Naomi looked away.

"But, *Naomi*...a *wedding* and a reunion with your mother after *twenty-some years*? I do not know if one could consider *those* as acceptable excuses." Hiram looked down at her with absolute seriousness, paused and walked away leaving her with a flash of his wide grin and a wink.

Naomi relaxed and took another sip. She shook her head. "Hiram McDonnally, you are positively priceless." She smiled and left to find her husband. The reception ended with the crowd forming a circle around the bride and groom. They sang Auld Lang Syne, led by Hiram's resonant voice.

The neighbors returned to their homes and although the wedding gifts traditionally were opened in advance, Naomi and Edward chose to open them with family after the reception. However, the Wheaton girls were adamant about having the gift from their family to be opened before they left with the Dugans. Jeanie handed the small box tied with a blue bow to Naomi.

"Thank you girls. Although your parents could not be with us today, we enjoy their presence with your smiling faces." Each of the girls smiled proudly.

"Then open it, Mrs. Donnally," Jeanie insisted.

Naomi cracked the lid and peeked inside with Edward. "Girls it is lovely," Naomi lifted the fine silver Luckenbooth pin from the box.

"It was from our mother and father's weddin'," Wilmoth said proudly.

The girls nodded in unison.

"We thank you and your family and I have the perfect place for it," Edward announced. He took the pin and pinned it to the quilt.

"Thank you." Naomi gave each of the girls a grateful hug and kiss.

Next, Naomi lifted the lid of the large box embossed with silver and blue bells from the Zigmann family. Her heart quickened with anticipation of the unknown surprise that lay beneath the crinkled white paper. Edward watched impatiently as his wife gently removed the wrapping to reveal the leather case. Naomi's eyes twinkled with curiosity.

"Albert, Eloise, *what* is this?"

Albert smiled proudly and insisted, "Open it and see."

Naomi unlatched the brass closures under the direct inspection of the five Wheaton girls.

"Hurry, Mrs. McDonnally!" Marvel exclaimed.

"Please make haste, I cannot bear it any longer," Wilmoth whispered.

"Yes, Naomi!" Guillaume spoke with excitement, anxious to see her reaction. He then recoiled in his chair with embarrassment, as the other adults looked to him with surprise for the outburst.

Naomi slowly lifted the case lid while Jeanie, imagining the contents to be a medical case of sorts, peeked over the edge.

"Are ya to be a doctor, Mrs. Donnally?" Jeanie asked.

"Edward certainly provided you with the experience to be a proficient nurse," Hiram replied.

Edward nodded in agreement. Naomi peered into the case and fell back in her chair with shock.

"Albert, Eloise, I cannot believe it!"

Jeanie studied the mysterious gift and inquired, "What would it be?"

Naomi gently lifted the beautifully hand-crafted, musical instrument and replied in awe, "It is a Volkszither."

"A what zither?" Corinne asked.

"It is a..." Naomi dropped her head and began to sob in receiving the generous gift. Edward put his arm around her shoulders.

Hiram felt the familiar inclination to comfort her, as he did at the church, but left the responsibility to Edward. Jeanie, too, immediately responded to Naomi's reaction and walked over to the Zigmanns to take Albert's hand.

"Dunna worry, Mr. Zigmann. *I* think it is lovely gift."

Naomi raised her head and wiped her tears with Edward's offered handkerchief.

"No, Jeanie, yer misunderstandin," Harriet explained, "those are tears of happiness. And this is a musical harp o' sorts."

"I ne'er cried when I was happy," Jeanie said, looking confused.

"Someday, you shall," Hiram broke in.

All eyes met his and it was silent.

"The perfect gift," Beatrice said, "Naomi has always loved music."

Jeanie shook her head and then ran her tiny fingers over the smooth wooden body. "It is verra bonnie."

"Keep yer little fingers to yerself, now," Harriet commanded.

Naomi looked to the Zigmann family, "I do not know what to say."

Corinne whispered to Naomi, "Say 'thank you'."

Naomi withheld her amusement to Corinne's suggestion. "Yes, thank you, from the bottom of my heart." Jeanie and Corinne smiled at one another, proud that Naomi had come to her senses.

"It is wonderful, Mummy," Allison said smiling at Guillaume.

"You said that you always wanted to play an instrument," Eloise explained, "so, Albert ordered it from his cousin's shop in Germany."

"You cannot imagine how grateful I am for your thoughtfulness," Naomi stared in disbelief at her new acquisition. She removed a small scrap of paper from beneath the strings. "What is this?" She read it aloud. "*I Naomi McDonnally do hereby promise to practice this instrument and accompany Albert Zigmann in concert. Signed...*" She looked to Albert. "I shall sign it tomorrow."

"It is a fairly simple instrument to play, Mrs. McDonnally. You depress the chords and strum," Albert explained.

"Play it, Mrs. McDonnally," Marvel insisted.

Naomi positioned the fine instrument with Albert's help and strummed one chord.

The Wheaton girls looked at one another with wonder. "More!" they said in unison.

Albert cut in, "A good musician practices before he, or *she* performs publically."

"Aye," Joseph agreed.

Naomi carefully put the present back in its case.

"This is for the groom," Albert handed an envelope to Edward.

"This is for both of you," Guillaume handed Naomi a small book of poetry entitled, *Holmes Birthday Book*.

"Thank you, Guillaume. Poetry from *you*— of course." Naomi opened the book and read, "*January. The cheerful fire-light's glow streamed through the casement o'er the spectral snow; here while the night-wind wreaked its frantic will on the loose ocean and the rock-bound hill.* Beautiful, Guillaume. Look Edward, there is poetry or prose for each day of the year."

Edward nodded, and then excitedly opened the envelope. "Capital!" Edward exclaimed pulling out a dozen postage stamps.

"I removed them from letters from the relatives in Germany," Eloise commented.

"I am delighted. Thank you and I, too, shall enjoy Naomi's gift when she serenades me," he said dreamily.

"Poor Mr. Donnally. All he got was some ol' stamps," Jeanie complained to her sister Corinne.

Harriet overheard and began corralling the girls. "We need to get this brood tucked in for the night. Come along girls, we need to be fetchin' yer sister, Dara." Jeanie gave Marvin a quick smile while Harriet ushered the girls out of the room. "Remember, I shall be deliverin' a dozen jars of fresh preserves this summer for yer gift!" Harriet called as they left.

"Thank you! We are looking forward to them!" Edward called back.

The opening of the gifts continued.

"Open mine, now," Sophia insisted, handing them her gift, wrapped cleverly in two linen dinner napkins.

"You open this one, Edward," Naomi handed it to him.

Upon seeing the brightly painted candlesticks, Edward proclaimed, "Sophia, you have made your great uncle a very happy man, indeed. How did you know? Why only a few weeks past, I broke one of the crystal candlesticks when that dreadful wheeled chair caught the edge of the tablecloth."

"Yes, these are quite lovely, Sophia," Naomi added turning them over. "The colors and Swedish designs are so cheerful. Exactly what one would want to be greeted with first thing in the morning."

Rahzvon smiled to himself with the memory of Sophia's unexpected concern for the candles when their lives were at risk in the tree at Grimwald.

"I have waited long enough," Hiram announced, handing Edward his gift.

Naomi and Edward quickly opened the oddly shaped package. They removed an expertly made wooden stepstool with steps ascending from both sides. Naomi read the attached tag.

"*May you reach for your dreams together, but never any higher than this stool—NO MORE LADDERS!*"

Everyone laughed as Hiram apologized for his less than poetic attempt.

"Sturdy," Edward commented with satisfaction.

"Yes, very," Naomi agreed.

However, for the bride and groom, the stool symbolized more than Hiram had suggested. They clasped hands remembering the day on which Naomi hid Edward in the chimney on the stool, out of Nathan's view, and the day Edward proposed marriage when Naomi fell from the same stool, borrowed from McDonnally Manor. Henry's sons were equally thrilled with the gift and took turns climbing on it.

"And this may help you reach your dreams with a little less pain," Hiram handed Edward an ivory envelope. Naomi and Edward looked curiously at one another as Edward opened it. They read it and smiled up at the benefactor.

"Hiram, old man, you sly fox..."

"I feel as though I am dreaming," Naomi said excitedly.

Hiram sat back with a satisfied grin. Everyone immediately assumed that the gift was monetary in nature and of an exorbitant amount, until Naomi spoke.

"My *own* lady-in-waiting and a cottage for Mother, to be built on the estate?" Naomi turned and hugged her shocked parent.

The room buzzed with interest.

"Lady-in-waiting?" Allison asked.

"Aye, my extraordinary nephew took it upon himself to hire a personal maid for my wife and has paid her wages until our first anniversary," Edward left his chair to shake hands and embrace Hiram.

"Hiram, this is so very generous," Naomi joined Edward and stood on tiptoe to kiss Hiram's cheek.

"Only the best for my favorite Aunt and Uncle," Hiram said proudly.

Edward sat back feeling a little disturbed that Hiram had taken the initiative to provide for *his* wife and *her* mother.

Everyone resumed their seats when Allison asked again, "Who is this woman?"

"Yes, love, who have you hired?" Abigail inquired nervously.

Hiram leaned back in his chair with a smug grin. "I have to admit, I did not have to look too far. I found her right here in the village. I came up with this idea only recently."

"I know," Sophia guessed, "Agnes Murray! She has been seeking employment."

"No, not Miss Murray."

"Then who, Uncle?" Sophia asked, desperately.

"You have all met her," Hiram hinted.

Everyone searched their brains for the answer to the riddle.

"Enough, Uncle, tell us!" Sophia demanded.

"Yes, tell us!" Guillaume blurted out, and then withered in his chair.

"I am surprised at all of you. I have hired the lovely, Miss Dunmore."

Guillaume shot up in his chair, "Trina?" His eyes widened with terror.

The deafening silence in the room fully disarmed Hiram. He glanced around his audience, sensing the unexpected doom that his announcement created.

Sophia stared at Allison, whose nails were imprinting into Guillaume's forearm. While Rahzvon watched him grimace, Eloise, wrung her hands and Albert closed his eyes and sighed. Henry stared at the floor, refusing to make contact with his wife, which obviously disturbed her, and Naomi and Edward looked worried at one another.

While everyone seemed to be overwrought with the possibility of Trina becoming a permanent Lochmoor Glen fixture, Daniel's thoughts were elsewhere. He, like Edward, was troubled that his friend was to provide a home for the woman in his life. *She shall be here when I visit Abigail...but,* I

was to give her a home...with me o'er the shop.
However, Daniel realized that a home in London
would be impossible—Beatrice would never return
with Cecil present.

Having no knowledge of Guillaume's history
with Trina, Beatrice joined Hiram in his confusion.
Abigail immediately saw the necessity to remove
Hiram from the room and explain his incredible
error in judgment.

"Hiram, dear, may I have a word with you in
the kitchen?" Abigail said, tugging on his sleeve.
Dumbfounded, he got up and followed her through
the hall. When they reached the kitchen, Abigail
exploded without thought to the other guests.

"Hiram Geoffrey McDonnally, have you gone
quite mad? Do you ever think before you act? Did
you ever stop to think, for one moment, that you
should get *references* before you hired that
woman?"

Hiram knitted his brows in contempt, as
Abigail continued.

"Did you confide in me, your future wife
before you made this disastrous decision that shall
ruin, who knows *how many lives*? " Abigail stared
up at him with her hands on her hips. "You may be
a big man, Mr. McDonnally, but I sometime wonder
if you shall ever grow up! Now, what are you going
to do? I ask you, what are you going to do? I shall
tell you what you are going to do. You are going to
march back in there and—"

"Mind your sharp tongue, woman!" Before
she could refute, he scooped her up and carried her
with long deliberate strides to the parlor.

"Hiram, what are you doing? Put me down!"

His eyes were ablaze with fury as he entered
the parlor and dropped Abigail in the overstuffed

chair. She jerked herself into a more appropriate position and folded her arms, pouting when he spoke.

"No one move. No one is leaving this room until I receive an explanation for this bizarre behavior!"

Chapter XII

"Honor Defended"

"Ah! My faults like thorns are,
But cannot they be
Hidden 'neath the flower
Of my love for thee?"

—Robert Argyle Campbell

"What could be so monumentally wrong with my decision to hire Miss Dunmore?" Hiram bellowed. "I thought that it was an *unselfish* gesture."

The guests did not respond.

"Edward?" Hiram snapped.

"Perhaps we should discuss this in the library?" Edward suggested calmly.

"Nay, I am not leaving this room. My decision has obviously affected everyone, with the exception to Beatrice—who is apparently in the dark as much as I am on this subject."

"Hiram, the matter is of a delicate nature. That is the only reason that I suggested we discuss it elsewhere," Edward said quietly, knowing Hiram's response to Guillaume's involvement.

Hiram looked around the room. No one dared make eye contact with him. He clenched his teeth and gave a quick nod to Edward. He walked to the library with Edward close behind.

"Have a seat, Hiram," Edward suggested when they entered the room.

"Edward, who is this woman?"

"Trina Dunmore is an acquaintance of Guillaume Zigmann."

"Zigmann, again! He has vexed me more than any man on this earth!"

"Remember now, Hiram, Guillaume *did* help save your life and assist in capturing Dirth and MacGill."

"Why does it matter, if Guillaume is acquainted with her?" Hiram asked, peeved.

"It is a wee complicated."

"Is it not always, with Zigmann?"

"Hiram, Guillaume was engaged to Trina. She returned...uh... to stake her claim."

Hiram started laughing, "She has come to Lochmoor to take Zigmann from Allison? Hah, I think that I have done Allison a favor. Perhaps Allison shall abandon that relationship and find someone more suitable."

"Hiram, you are not being fair to Guillaume."

"Fair to Guillaume? That lad ended my relationship with Elizabeth!"

Edward's expression changed dramatically.

Abigail's voice blared behind Hiram.

"And to think that I was in there defending you—explaining how you were innocent! Go, go back to London! Find her! I am no better than Guillaume. I, too, am responsible for Elizabeth leaving you!" Abigail shouted and ran down the hall and out of the front door.

Edward yanked on Hiram's arm to turn him around and looked him straight in the eye.

"This is *my* wedding day, mine and Naomi's and *nothing* is going to spoil it. Do you hear me? No one shall hold you wholly responsible for this. Trina knew exactly what she was doing when she accepted your offer. The problem is between Guillaume and Trina and it is up to Guillaume to resolve this situation. We are grateful for the thoughtful gesture, but this disruption has taken enough of our day. No more! Go and fetch Abigail, now! Bring her back for dinner and you had better appear to be the most loving couple in Lochmoor," Edward took a breath, and straightened his jacket, "other than Naomi and myself."

Hiram strained to withhold any negative commentary and turned to leave. "As you say, Master McDonnally," Hiram walked down the hall and out the door.

Hiram saw Abigail's silhouette as she moved furiously down the road. He ran to catch up to her and soon was pacing her. He walked several steps alongside of her before he spoke.

"Please stop, Abigail?"

"Go back to Elizabeth," Abigail retaliated and kept moving with Hiram next to her.

"I could. She *did* tell me where to find her when she visited my flat in Town."

Abigail was furious at the news that he had spoken recently with Elizabeth, but continued without a rebuttal.

When they finally reached McDonnally Manor, where she and her brother resided as Hiram's guests, Abigail bolted for the portico. With several long strides, Hiram reached it before her, blocking the door. He folded his arms across his chest.

"Do you love her?" Abigail asked non-challantly.

"Aye, and I am in love with Allison, and Delilah, and Harriet Dugan and Eloise and, of course, Trina Dunmore. That is why I hired her."

"I think Miss Dunmore has done quite enough," Abigail looked away, with her hands on her hips.

"Surrender, Abby," he demanded. Abigail would not look at or speak to him.

Hiram walked over and stood over her.

"Can you not look at me? Nay, you cannot, for fear that I may see the love in your eyes, which betrays you. Aye, I had every opportunity to resolve my difficulties with Elizabeth, but I did not. In fact, she knew immediately that her visit was in vain. *Now...* tonight is a celebration and I promised

Edward that I would return with you and we *would* behave favorably."

Abigail turned toward the road and began walking back to Brachney Hall. Hiram followed, satisfied with her decision to return. Neither spoke a word on the long walk back to Brachney Hall, until they reached the door and Abigail stopped. Hiram reached for the door, and then retracted his hand. A minute passed. Abigail mumbled some indiscernible comment.

"I did not hear what you said," he asked.

"She actually visited you in London with hopes of...?"

"She did."

"You sent her away?" Abigail asked pointedly.

"I did. Shall we join the others?"

"All right..."

Hiram opened the door and escorted Abigail to the dining room where there seemed to be some commotion over the seating arrangements. Naomi was busy shuffling the place cards in a frenzy. When she saw that Hiram and Abigail had returned she smiled with relief, threw the cards over her shoulder and announced, "Everyone, sit anywhere you choose!"

As the dinner progressed, numerous toasts were given to the bride and groom and Trina's name was never mentioned. Hiram and Abigail sat directly across from each other. During the meal, Hiram was engaged in conversation with Henry and Albert, while Abigail listened to Pearl's account of her first meeting with her husband. On several occasions, Hiram and Abigail's eyes met with hope to resolve their differences privately.

Soon Pearl's ramblings and Albert's anecdotes fell on deaf ears. Hiram made the first move and excused himself from the table. Abigail, shortly, followed suit. With the myriad of topics of conversation, their absence went unnoticed. Abigail walked slowly down the hall.

"Hiram, where are you?" she whispered in the dimly lit corridor. She continued toward the library, suspecting that he would be there in the room where they first declared their love. She continued, then stopped and went on to the kitchen *He must learn that I am not as predictable as he may believe.*

Abigail strolled steadily to the kitchen where she moved a few trays around and sampled a few of the afters left from the reception. Eloise startled her, when she entered the room.

"Oh, hello, Eloise."

"Miss O'Leardon."

"Eloise, are you comfortable with the situation?"

"With Trina?"

"No, I was referring to Daniel with Naomi's mother."

Eloise sat down on the ladder-back chair.

"At first, I did not know how I felt. But now that I have met Beatrice, I am comfortable around Daniel, for the first time. I can honestly say that I am very pleased. For months, I felt responsible for Daniel's solitary life... guilty for having deprived him of the happiness that I found with Albert." Eloise stood up. "Now, Daniel is truly happy again; you can see it, every time he looks at her. I know that look. He used to look at me like that. Yes, Miss O'Leardon, I do believe your brother and Beatrice are meant for one another."

"I am very pleased to hear you say that, Eloise."

"Now, I believe that there is an uncommonly handsome gentleman waiting in the shadows of the library for you, Miss O'Leardon."

"Yes, I believe you are right." She turned to leave.

Eloise touched her arm. "Thank you, I needed to share my feelings about Daniel to someone."

Abigail gave a quick nod and left. Within a few steps, she was at the threshold of the library. The room was dark with exception to the stream of starlight pouring through the windows that faced the pond. Abigail stepped in.

"Hiram? Answer me. I know that you are here." Abigail moved slowly around the table situated in the center of the room, straining to examine the corners. "Hiram? We cannot stay in here forever?"

"Why not?" His voiced whispered behind her.

Abigail turned into his arms.

Hiram reached behind her.

"Hiram, what are you doing?"

"You do not need this," he pulled the clip from her hair. Her red curls fell down over her shoulders.

"I am cutting it, you know. It *is* the latest fashion," Abigail teased.

"And I am shaving my head."

Abigail reached up and pulled gently on one of his black silken curls.

"I think not," she whispered.

Approaching voices in the hall initiated Hiram's move to pull Abigail behind the opened door with him.

"Time is short, love. Shall we apologize, now?" Hiram leaned down, kissed her forehead, then her cheek and then finalized his apology with a passionate kiss, which left Abigail breathless.

Abigail rested her head on his chest, "Perhaps we *can* stay here forever?"

"Edward might find our presence a wee distracting when he is studying his stamp collection."

Then they heard Edward, standing only a few feet away in the hall, addressing Eloise. "Eloise, have you seen Hiram and Abigail?"

The missing couple stood motionless, listening. Suspiciously, Eloise did not answer and Edward did not continue his inquiry.

"Hiram, Eloise knows we are in here... in the dark. I am so embarrassed. You know Edward, he shall tell *everyone*," Abigail whispered.

"I can light the lamp," Hiram proposed.

"It is too late for that. We have to get out of here without them noticing. We can escape out the window."

"Abby, do you really expect us to climb out the window like a couple of bandits? I think we should stay here and enjoy the atmosphere," he ran his fingers across her neck.

"Hiram! What about defending my honor? Do you want me to be humiliated?"

"You are overly concerning yourself. We are all adults."

"Hiram McDonnally, you get me out through that window right now!" she whispered.

"All right, come along," Hiram relented.

He pushed the sash a few inches further, and then turned.

"Listen, Abby."

"I do not hear anything."

"Nor do I."

"Do you think that they left?" she asked.

"To where? I sense something is not quite right, hurry." Hiram climbed out the window. Abigail reached down to him and he pulled her through down to the ground.

"This way, Abby, around to the front door and enter, as though we stepped out for a few minutes."

Hiram took Abigail's hand and crept around the corner of the house only to be met with a dozen smiling faces.

Edward greeted the shocked escapees, "Fire in the library, Hiram?" Everyone laughed at the blushing couple. "From the condition of your faces, I would say that temperatures were rising in there! Now, who is foolish in opening the window, Hiram?" Edward mocked.

Eventually the barrage of jokes ended with everyone relocating to the banks overlooking the pond. Equipped with a half dozen quilts and blankets, the couples spread them on the ground to sit in the starlight of the spring eve. Eloise snuggled under Albert's arm while contentedly observing Beatrice and Daniel talking quietly together. Guillaume and Allison, pondering the dilemma involving Trina, sat directly behind Naomi and Edward who were identifying the various constellations. Sophia and Rahzvon, on the other hand, chose to walk Rusty and Heidi for the pup's late night swim.

Hiram and Abigail left the group, walking arm in arm, and disappeared to the other side of the pond.

"Where the storms that we feel
in this cold world should cease,
And our hearts like thy waters,
Be mingled in peace."

—Thomas Moore

Chapter XIII

"Seeking Answers"

"This is the hour of Lead—
Remembered, if outlived,
As freezing persons, recollect the snow—
First—Chill—then Stupor—then the letting go—"

—Emily Dickinson

Three days after the wedding, Hiram and Abigail were enjoying a game of cards in the parlor.

"Well, love, shall we take a turn around the grounds while the night is still young?" Hiram asked getting up from the table.

"Yes, I think that I should like to stretch my legs a bit." Hiram escorted her to the hall and opened the front door. He stepped out into the portico, when Abigail turned to leave.

"One minute, I want to fetch my wrap from the parlor." Abigail left when Hiram saw a man on horseback coming up the drive. The man stopped and dismounted.

"Good evening, sir, may I introduce myself, I am Captain Latimer." The blonde, fair-skinned middle-aged soldier stood tall before Hiram.

"Hiram McDonnally, how may I be of service to you?"

"I understand that Miss Abigail O'Leardon is visiting here."

Hiram's welcoming smile disappeared. He looked at the perfect soldier with suspicion. Hiram was preparing to announce his relationship with Abigail when his future bride appeared next to him.

"Roland, how wonderful to see you! It has been months!" Abigail exclaimed.

Hiram glared at the interaction of the *too friendly* acquaintances in his doorway.

"Abby, nearly a year. I have missed you! You are looking positively smashing!"

Hiram sneered, *Smash you, I would like to squash you like a bug.*

"Thank you, and you, Roland, make quite the handsome soldier," Abigail cooed.

"I have been promoted to Captain," he said proudly.

"I am not at all surprised. You excelled in every class at school. How is everyone? Oh, what am I thinking? Hiram, we should invite Roland to come in," Abigail suggested. Hiram hesitated in complying.

"Actually, it is a marvelous night for a stroll. If you do not mind, Abby, would you care to join me?" Roland asked.

"Looks like rain," Hiram quickly interjected, "I think you should come in." The captain and Abigail looked to the clear sky with confusion. Abigail ignored Hiram's discontent expression and agreed to join the captain.

"I shall have her back shortly, old chap." Roland smiled and offered Abigail his arm. Abigail gave a little wave of her hand.

With incontestable jealousy, Hiram remained in the portico, watching his newly acquired fiancé disappear down the road on the arm of the unexpected apparition from her past. To Hiram, Captain Latimer represented, not only a threat to his relationship, but a reminder of his failure to meet the McDonnally expectations to continue the line of serving men.

Hiram closed the door, walked into the parlor and stood silent, feeling forsaken and angry. He looked up to the portrait of his father in uniform and grasped the back of the rocking chair.

"I have been promoted to a *captain*," Hiram grumbled.

Hiram got a grip on his emotions and released his grip on the chair, realizing that Abigail loved him and had agreed to be his wife. He took a deep breath and walked to the hall mirror to straighten his jacket. He looked solemnly at his reflection. "Control, man, keep control."

The next half hour was one of the longest of his life. He chose one of Emerson's volumes from the study, returned to the parlor and lit the kindling in the fireplace. He sat, trying desperately to relax and concentrate on Emerson's advice. He quickly abandoned the writings to consider a response for when Abigail returned. Despite his antagonism, he felt it demanded that he not reveal any concern for her relationship with the intruder. He paused, staring at the vase of flowers on the table before him, recognizing it as one of the many remaining from the wedding. He studied it for a moment noting that several of the cut flowers were fresh and intact. However, those flowers of a different variety had lost most of their petals, which had fallen to the table. Projecting from his dilemma, the contrast struck him as disturbing and unjust. He began pacing madly across the room, vacillating between insidious, jealous thoughts and the planned dialog.

Hiram held his breath at the sound of the door creaking. Abigail's appearance in the archway and the sound of diminishing hooves provided him with a needed moment of relief.

"Did you miss me?" Abigail asked flirtatiously.

"You were not gone long enough to be missed," Hiram said in a disinterested tone, filling a goblet with water at the small table, to steady his nerves.

"Roland looked quite handsome in his uniform," she commented. Hiram's fingers tightened around the stem of the glass.

She walked over to Hiram, reached up and ran her palms over his jacket lapels. "I think that *you* would look finer, by far, donning a uniform."

Hiram half-smiled and took a drink. "Well, you shall never know, shall you?"

"Perhaps not, unless Scotland is called to war, and then you would naturally enlist," Abigail responded matter-of-factly.

"I would not," Hiram stated firmly.

"Surely, you jest."

Not you, too? Hiram, annoyed, looked to the window to escape her focus. "It is *not* a matter of which I address with humor." Hiram lowered the glass to the table. He walked away returning both hands to the back of the rocking chair.

Abigail stepped back in astonishment.

"Hiram, do you not honor and respect your country?" she scorned.

Hiram tightened his grip on the chair, fighting the urge to explode.

"Abigail, why are *you* asking me these questions? What did *he* say to you?" Hiram countered.

"He said nothing. I would like an answer." The volume of Abigail's voice increased, "Why would you not fight to defend your country?"

"Why would I not kill like the *fine* Captain? Is that what you are asking?" Hiram shot back.

"Roland is an honorable soldier. It takes courage to serve! Perhaps, you believe that your wealth excuses you from the *loathsome* duties of a soldier?"

"I choose to support my country by other means, Abigail. Let us discuss something more pleasant?" Hiram forced a smile and sat down in the chair next to the fireplace.

Abigail walked over and examined his appealing face with disgust. "Mr. McDonnally, do not tell me that you do not desire to risk damaging that perfect face?" she said in contempt.

Hiram flew from the chair.

"Your *perfect* soldier shows no sign of suffering at the front lines!"

"Dare you criticize, Roland? It is *you* that we are discussing and is quite apparent by your refusal to respond, that the great Master McDonnally is a coward!" Abigail charged.

"Coward! You think that I am a coward? I have had ample opportunities to kill and I did not need a uniform to prove it to the world!"

Hiram continued as the memories poured forth, "I could have killed the blasted shipmate who stole a year of my earnings, the ruddy fool who attempted to rob the clock shop or the detestable men who cornered Delilah in the shed! I was twice their size! And Dirth, aye, *Dirth,* who lay helpless beneath my blade! I could have killed all of them—everyone who sinned against me and the ones I loved! But, I did not, I left them to the courts—because I chose *not* to take the life of another man! I would think that you would respect my decision."

Fuming, he walked away from her to the window.

"*Respect?* Yes, and Dirth! So, you had the opportunity to eliminate every possibility of that beast terrifying me again, and you did not?" she screamed following him.

Hiram swung around, "You wanted me to *kill* the man?" he shouted down at her.

"I do not know! But someday he shall be free to return! And shall you defend me? No! I shan't ever be safe as long as I stay with you and I shan't share the name of a coward!"

Hiram stepped forward, looming over her, "This is *his* fault! You are refusing to be my wife because some arrogant, uniformed fraud, who perches behind a desk, *tainted* my doorstep!"

"I find your attitude toward the men who protect our country *intolerable*," Abigail shouted.

"*Your country?* This is not *your* country!"

"I am glad it is *not,* if it is depending on men like you to protect it. You cannot even protect *one woman!* Cowardice is *one* weakness that I cannot tolerate in a man!" she shook her head, angrily. "I shall not stay another night in this house! The engagement is over!"

"Do you have the audacity to think for one second that I could honor a wife who would not *respect* my decisions? Get out, Abigail!" He flipped over the rocking chair and then slammed his fist into the wall, accompanied by the sound of crumbling plaster.

Abigail turned to the hall where her brother stood in shock of the altercation.

"Daniel, drive me to the inn! I shall be accompanying Captain Latimer back to London in the morning!"

"Aye, go with your blasted *Captain!* And go back to your *own* country!" Hiram bellowed.

"And your temper is *abominable!*" Abigail retorted.

"You, my fine woman, bring out the worst in *any* man!" he called out after her as she marched upstairs to pack.

Hiram snatched the vase of flowers, hurled it at his father's portrait and kicked the table into the fireplace.

Daniel shuddered at the sound of the breaking glass, falling to the mantle and closed his eyes in disappointment with the behavior of both parties. He stood facing Hiram, now flushed and breathing hard. They stared at each other in disbelief, for only an hour earlier they were celebrating Hiram and Abigail's lifelong commitment.

With a moment of hesitation, Daniel offered, "Hiram, I agree, your honor as a McDonnally shan't require a battlefield to be defendin' it. It is Abby's misfortune to believe that it does. I shall speak wit' her."

"Do not waste your time," Hiram added wearily, staring blankly toward the floor.

Daniel went upstairs and entered the bedroom where Abigail was pulling clothing from the drawers of the chest.

"Do not say a word, Daniel! I know that he is your dearest friend, but I shan't ever marry him."

"Abigail, only an hour past, ye were content to spend the rest o' yer life wit' Hiram."

"I did not know him, then." She stuffed two skirts into her bag.

"Yer bein' rash, Abby. Ya need to speak wit' Hiram again."

Abigail stopped packing and turned defiantly toward her brother.

"Daniel, how would you react if Beatrice told you that she was adamantly opposed to reading and she believed all books should be destroyed?"

"That is ridiculous, Abby."

"Ridiculous or not, you know very well that you would not marry her. Hiram has always known, from the first day when we met in your flat, that I have no tolerance for cowardice! I have lost respect for him and I shan't marry a man who I do not respect. His lack of spine gives me cause to fear for my safety."

"Uh, *Abby*!" Daniel threw up his arms in frustration. "Ya misunderstand. Hiram is anythin' but a coward...ya loved the man!"

"He is *not* the man who I thought he was!" She continued cramming her clothing into her trunk.

"Ya shall come to regret this, Abby!"

"No, Daniel, you shall be the only one who regrets our ending this relationship. Nothing more needs to be said—it is over! I shall be ready to leave in a few minutes."

Daniel watched her, feeling frustrated and disgusted with his sister's hasty decision.

"At least, give him an opportunity to explain," Daniel demanded. "How can ya *not* understand? Not ev'ry man can or should be a soldier. Hiram has a commitment to his faith."

Abigail snatched the small bag and pointed to her trunk.

"His commitment to his faith is obviously *greater* than his commitment to me."

With that unexpected statement, Daniel ceased his politicking.

Hiram left the remains of the parlor with mixed emotions of fury, outrage and disappointment. He kicked past the destroyed table, stomped upstairs to his bedroom and slammed the door. He sat down on the bed, trying desperately to comprehend what had occurred. He lowered his head, folded his hands and stared at the floor for several minutes, attempting to interpret the marked change in Abigail's behavior. He then lay back, staring into the vast darkness, feeling lost and helpless in the familiar void of loneliness.

The door closing down the hall. Footsteps on the stairs.

His motionless body became tense and his breathing quickened. He listened and waited. For the next two hours, he prayed for Abigail to return. She did not.

It became all too real; it *was* over—all his hopes and dreams were gone. He lay still as though he were made of stone, unable to move.

I do not understand... why did I have to struggle to win her affections, when you *knew that she would never accept me for the person I am?*

He turned to the wall.

Why did it happen again?

His thoughts skipped randomly to the women of his past—Naomi, devastated after their meeting in the parlor, Allison, heart-broken when he ended their friendship and Elizabeth at flat Number Eight. Then, Abby.

He realized the irony of the first disastrous proposal dinner with her and the wonder of the second attempt, when he lay in the ditch with her. A vision of Abby walking away with the captain quickly appeared. Hiram stared at the wall, defiantly justifying the hypocrisy; yes, he had reprimanded Abigail for her jealousy of Delilah, but his antagonism for the intruding soldier, was apparently well founded.

He moved restlessly, haunted by Abigail's wrath and *his* that ended in the inevitable destruction of his home and his future. Hiram defensively closed his eyes, seeking more pleasant thoughts, trailing back to Naomi and Edward's wedding. His eyes blinked open to reality, with his envying their new life together and brooding sadly over his futile plans for the honeymoon at Deeside with Abigail.

He turned over, unbearably disappointed, that once again, life had left him alone.

All of them—Abigail, Naomi, and Elizabeth chose to leave me. Only one... only one, never hurt me and she is gone forever.

Livia, my Livy.

The dark agony of her desperate cry at her departure, painfully spliced its way back into his memory. The anger and sorrow of Abigail's reproach faded, as he was overcome, once again, with the grieving loss of Livia Nichols.

At that very moment, at Brachney Hall, Naomi woke with a start. With an uneasy feeling she sat up, staring at the bed canopy.

"Edward, are you awake?"

"Well, I am certainly not asleep."

"Something is wrong, I can feel it."

"It is probably your maternal feelings toward the Wheaton children. Tragic situation."

"Yes, maybe." She lay back. "I cannot imagine what are to become of those five, sweet, little girls. Who knows how long it shall be until Maryanne recovers from her illness and Bruce is well enough to travel. I guess we should be thankful that she visited Bruce so that she, too, was admitted and treated. How can the Dugans manage with all five cramped into that one bedroom? Tavy moved out to the shed to sleep."

"I wonder why the Dugans had the girls spend the night at their cottage," Edward asked.

Naomi turned toward him. "You know Harriet was Maryanne's dearest friend. Why Harriet was like a mother to her. Naturally, she would take the girls."

"Naomi, I was simply questioning why the Dugans did not spend the night at the Wheaton farm with the girls."

"Is it not obvious? Harriet wanted to spare the girls of the trauma of returning to the farm with their parents absent."

"Leave it to Harriet to think of all the details. She is an extraordinary woman."

Naomi laid back. "She certainly is. She helped Maryanne after every birth."

"However, Joseph is probably at his wits end. He is not too fond of children. Have they contacted the kin?"

"There is none. Bruce was an orphan and Maryanne was an only child. Maryanne's mother is living in a home for the blind in Ireland," Naomi explained.

"Tragic. Tragic situation. Any cousins in the clan?"

"Only two, a young man of eighteen, a sailor, I believe, and a cousin in Ireland who has eight children of her own... Such a small house."

"Joseph probably feels like he is in a packed herring tin," Edward said sympathetically.

"Harriet is not young."

"Neither is Joseph. Pray for them Naomi. The good Lord shall provide for them."

"Yes, Edward...goodnight."

"Goodnight, love." Edward leaned over and kissed her.

Naomi rolled over with not only concern for the Wheaton children, but for the inexplicable feeling that she had experienced earlier.

The next morning, Naomi washed and dressed after finding her husband missing. She started downstairs when she heard footsteps in the bedroom down the hall.

"Edward?"

"In here, Naomi."

Naomi entered the bedroom and saw Edward standing in the middle of the room.

"What are you doing in here?"

"Measuring."

"Measuring what?"

"The floors."

"The floors?"

"For furniture. Do you think that they would each like their own room or prefer to bunk together?"

"*Bunk* together?"

"Cowboy talk. What do you think?"

"Edward, what are you suggesting?" Naomi asked cautiously.

"Naomi, would you, in good conscience, leave the Dugans to raise that brood when we are nearly twenty years younger and have this big empty home?"

Naomi flew into Edward's arms.

"Edward! Are you certain that you want to do this? There are five of them. One is only an infant and they are all *girls*." Naomi kissed him and nearly squeezed the breath out of him.

"However, being one in a house with three women, five girls and two female pets, I expect special attention. I may have to form an alliance with Dest," Edward said sounding defeated.

"I am certain, that you shall get more attention than you can bear. I have to tell Allison. Is she awake, yet?"

"No need to hurry, she already knows."

"You told her?" Naomi asked with surprise.

"No, she told me. Daughter *like* mother. 'When are you and Mummy going to take in the Wheaton girls?' were the first words out of her mouth, this morning."

"She *is* happy about it, is she not?"

"Immensely."

Edward placed his arm around Naomi's shoulders. She put hers around his waist and they walked downstairs to meet with Allison.

"You shall be wonderful with them, Edward."

"I can use the practice—you never know when these rooms shall be occupied in the future."

Chapter XIV

"The Keys"

"The Bravest—grope a little—
And sometimes hit a Tree
Directly in the forehead—
But as they learn to see—

Either the Darkness alter,
Or something in the sight
Adjust itself to Midnight—
And Life steps almost straight."

—Emily Dickinson

It was nearly eleven o'clock and the McDonnally mansion was quiet. Hiram drifted off after a severe self-evaluation of his inability to maintain a relationship with a woman or to understand the Father's plan for him. Abigail had checked into the inn, Daniel returned to the manor, and Sophia was tossing and turning trying to occupy her mind with something other than the charming young man in the barn. Out of sheer boredom, she picked up the copy of *Wind in the Willows* that Daniel had given to her to read to the Wheaton children. Within minutes, she became immersed in the world of Mr. Toad, Rat, Mole and Badger. When Mr. Toad entered the *Red Lion* café for a bite to eat, Sophia found the power of suggestion to be overwhelming and ventured down to the kitchen for some afters.

When she arrived, she prepared a small tray with a variety of tasty tidbits and was about to retire, when she saw a note pinned to Eloise's apron, hanging on the hook by the pantry. Sophia sat down the tray, removed it without any consideration to Eloise's privacy, and read it. In an instant moment of panic, Sophia, with no thought to her uncle's house rules, abandoned the tray and darted across the pasture in her nightgown. *It cannot be true! I shan't allow it!* she thought as she flew into the barn.

"Rahzvon, wake up!"

"Phia! What are you doing here and dressed like that?" Rahzvon asked fearfully, jumping from his bed of straw.

"I need to speak with you. It cannot wait until morning," she said catching her breath.

"Do you want me to be banished from this country, as well? Your uncle has the power to do it!"

"Oh stop quibbling, Uncle Hiram is asleep; he is not aware that I am here."

"I *do not* believe it. That man has a special sense—he shall discover that you are here and I shall be thrown to the road or worse!"

"You worry too much. Look up there, his room is dark." Sophia pointed to the window.

"Yes, he is *probably* on his way down here. *Go back* to the house, we can talk tomorrow."

Sophia defiantly stepped closer. "Rahzvon, you cannot shout orders at me like a servant!"

He looked down at her with his eyes blazing. "I am not shouting. We agreed to honor and respect your uncle's rules, *Sophia*."

"These are special circumstances. This is serious!"

"I could not agree more with you, so get out of here and get back to your room, before I *do* start shouting." He pointed to the door.

"I risked everything to come here and I am not leaving without answers!"

"Sophia, I am angry now. The only answer that you are getting out of me is, no!" He took her by the arm, leading her to the door when Sophia pulled away.

"Rahzvon Sierzik, you are the most disappreciative, brute that—"

"Inappreciative."

"Ungrateful man, I have ever known! I cannot, for the life of me, understand why I give you the slightest consideration?" She stormed over to the wall displaying the tack.

"Then do not, not *tonight*. I have finally earned your uncle's respect and I do not plan to lose it because of a foolish *whim*! So... *please* return to the house," he asked, softening his tone.

"Foolish whim?" Sophia shouted. "I dragged myself out of bed in concern of *your* well-being*!*"

"You may rest assured that I am healthy, well-fed and comfortable. Now, you may leave." He began moving her toward the door.

"Do you *have* to comment on my every remark? May I *please*, finish my explanation? Not that you deserve one," she said, fighting his efforts.

Rahzvon stopped, thoroughly frustrated and looked nervously toward the window. "Phia, a quarter hour has already past," he reported furiously.

"Ah. How do you know?" Sophia moved away toward the stalls. "Do you have a timepiece in your head?" she squinted, smirking at him.

"That is it! That was your last comment!" Rahzvon approached her.

"You stop right there or I shall scream," she demanded with a blocking motion of her hands.

Rahzvon stopped and took in a deep breath, trying to temper is anger. Sophia bravely marched over to him and looked up with disgust.

"You are *not* going to live at the inn."

"Is *that* why you are here?" he asked in disbelief.

"Answer me, Rahzvon!"

"I do not remember hearing a question, but *yes,* I *am* moving to the inn."

"You are *disserting* me?"

"No, I am not. My living at the inn shan't affect our *adoring* relationship. *However,* I may be blessed with a decent night of sleep."

"*Not affect our relationship?* I shall never see you again!"

"Phia, I *am* employed here. That is not going to change, *unless* your uncle finds you here."

"You did *not* ask me before you made that decision," she scolded.

"I am a man of free will. Good night, *Sophia.* I am going to sleep on this *great* bed of straw. I cannot *imagine* why I would consider sleeping in a featherbed at the inn. Stay if you like, but do not disturb me. I have a full day tomorrow."

He crawled back under the blanket and closed his eyes. Sophia stomped her foot in the dust.

"You are leaving because you want to spend as little time as possible with me! I am no fool!" She left the barn huffing and puffing.

Rahzvon opened his eyes, sat up burning with her grossly inaccurate accusation. He pulled off his shirt, whipped it to the dirt and fell back to his makeshift bed. Sophia marched on, mumbling to herself, through the garden to the back entrance. She reached to open the door when she received a heart-stopping shock.

The door was *locked.* She turned, pushed and pulled on the handle. *How can this be? No, I have to get back to my room!* She struggled with door several more times. *This cannot be happening! Uncle shall think that I was in the barn all night!*

She ran around to the front of the mansion watching for any open windows. Exhausted and panting she reached the front entrance, aware that the chances of it being unlocked were next to none. She tried the locked door and walked hopelessly back to the garden. She looked up at her uncle's window, noting that his room was still dark and began pacing.

I have to stop and think clearly. What are my choices? She looked at the looming door. *I need the key.* She took another turn past the shrubs. *That is it! I can go to the cottage and get the key from Eloise.*

She started for the gate and then paused.

At this hour, Eloise shan't answer the door. Guillaume would be fine, but not Albert. No, his loyalties lie with my uncle. He would report all of this without a second thought.

With that likelihood, she took cover behind the bushes. *There is no point in staying here. Uncle shall never believe that I was not in the barn.* She conceded, *I might as well leave Lochmoor with Rahzvon because after tonight, neither of us shall have a home.*

"No...no, he got me into this, he can get me out," Sophia muttered and headed back to the barn. She made a mad dash to the gate, praying that no one saw her. She entered the barn, walked over to where Rahzvon was sleeping and stood over him distracted by the excellent features of his moonlit face.

"Beautiful Creazna," he muttered the name of the princess who banished him.

Sophia's eyes narrowed, staring at the sleeping traitor.

"Do you desire for me to die young, SOPHIA?" Rahzvon asked opening his eyes.

Sophia startled, jumped back.

"It is fortunate for you, Mr. Sierzik, that I *knew* that you were aware of my presence. Creazna, *humph.*"

"*Phia,*" he sat up and shook his head, "*why* have you returned?"

"Rahzvon, you have to help me," she demanded.

"Tomorrow, I am tired," he fell back to his bed.

"Rahzvon, get up! Do you not understand? I am locked out of the house!"

Rahzvon sat up. "Locked *out?* How did that happen?" He stood up, fumbling to slip on his shirt. Sophia made a poor attempt to cover her eyes.

"It is over Phia. I knew it." He quickly began pulling on his boots. "He knows you are here and he locked you out," Rahzvon said shaking his head with despair. "And now, here you are...dressed like *that.*"

"Please stop saying that? It is not as though I am in a bathing suit. Besides, Uncle Hiram is much too vocal to lock me out. No," she folded her arms, "I think that it was Eloise. She had mentioned that she was going to read for a while in the study this evening. I wonder if she was reading Uncle Hiram's copy of *The Time Machine*. I could sure use one, now."

"A book, now?" Rahzvon asked, confused.

"No, a time machine."

"*Sophia*, will you please concentrate on the matter at hand."

"Perhaps Eloise left after I did." Sophia started to pace, then stopped.

"That is *right*, the door was unlocked when I left."

Now, Rahzvon was pacing.

"Rahzvon, you have to think of some way to help me, it is your responsibility."

"*My* responsibility?"

"If you would not have planned to move to the inn, I would not have read the note and I shan't be here tonight!"

He walked over to Sophia and looked down at her. "*Woman...*" his eyes flashed with warning.

She looked at him meekly, "I know, *vedriza mynoud tofmi.*"

She reached up and slid her hand down his cheek. "What about the *leslew zaward skichared?*"

Rahzvon moved her hand from his face, "If we do not get you *out* of here, your uncle shall see to it that we reach *chared* a lot sooner than we had expected. Now, do not touch me, you are distracting me. I have to think about this."

Sophia began pacing around the barn with him.

"Phia!"

"They say two pacers are better than one."

"They do not. Now, we need a place to put you—an acceptable place in your uncle's opinion."

"I could go to the Dugans and say that I want to help with the children."

Rahzvon stopped, "In your *nightdress?*"

Sophia rolled her eyes, "You think of a better idea, if you are so clever."

Rahzvon stopped and smiled.

"Ohh, no, Rahzvon. The last time you had that expression, we had to help Angus scrub the soot off of Duff." She walked over to the horse in his stall, "Poor boy," she reached over to pat its face.

"No, trust me, I have it, Phia!"

"What do you have?" she asked dubiously.

"The key!"

"*You* have had the key *all* this time?"

"No, not *that* key, the key to your Uncle Edward's home."

"You have the key to Brachney Hall?" Sophia's eyes widened.

"I do. It is right here."

He reached into the pocket of his trousers, removed the key and held it before her ecstatic face.

"Here, take it, your key to freedom! Naomi gave it to me so that I could let myself in the house, before she hired the servants."

Sophia grabbed it from his hand and admired it like a pearl in an oyster shell.

"That is fine, but do you expect me to walk there, alone, in the *dark*?"

"No, but we need to make haste. If your uncle wakens and finds *you* gone from your room and *me* absent from the barn, this trip shall be all for naught."

"What about my clothes, Rahzvon?"

"No, I am certainly not giving you any of mine. That got us into a peck of trouble the last time. Naomi shall provide you with something to wear."

"Yes, Naomi shall understand, she was young and in love, once."

"*Young and in love?* Was that what this mission was all about?" he mocked.

"We need to hurry," Sophia ignored his comment.

Rahzvon grinned and showed her the door.

"After you, m' lady."

When they reached the edge of the woods, Sophia stopped.

"Rahzvon, we have to take the road."

"We came this way because it is shorter than the pasture. You want to walk out on the road, wearing *that*?" he pointed to her gown.

Sophia took his hand and followed him into the woods. The path was more challenging than either had expected. Although they had travelled it by day dozens of times, the branches, stones and fallen limbs were not visible beneath the upper story foliage, blocking the celestial light.

This was not at all wise. The deeper we go the worse it gets, Rahzvon lamented.

Sophia's ears were acute, listening for some unknown man or beast preparing for attack. Rahzvon kept one hand outstretched feeling for branches the other with a tight grip on Sophia's.

"*Vedriza mynoud tofmi,*" he muttered under his breath.

"What did you say?"

"I said that this is absurd. Trouble seems to follow you everywhere. You are a female Guillaume Zigmann."

Sophia slipped her hand from his and backed away. "Is that what you think? So, that is the reason you are moving to the inn, because all I am is—"

"STOP!!" Rahzvon yelled at the top of his lungs.

Sophia withdrew in terror and froze to the sound of his voice echoing through the night.

Then it was silent.

"Rahzvon, *what* is it?" she whispered. "Is it a hole?"

He said nothing.

"Rahzvon? Are you there? Have you fallen?" she said fearfully.

"The only hole is that mouth of yours, Sophia, out of which a constant stream of nonsensical gibberish flows."

Sophia's mouth opened in shock.

"You yelled loud enough to wake up *all* of Lochmoor Glen, not to mention my uncle, because you did not want me to *talk*? *You* are a mad man!"

"You were not talking, you were rambling about foolish notions, insinuating that I do not care for you," he said in a controlled tone. "Yes, I am a mad man; there is no doubt in my mind. Anyone who would wander through the woods with the improperly dressed niece of Hiram McDonnally *in the middle of the night* can be nothing less than insane."

Sophia said nothing. Rahzvon could hear her backing further away from him.

"Phia, give me your hand...*Sophia.*"

The sounds from her movement were becoming more distant.

"Aghh!" she yelled.

"Phia, are you hurt? Answer me! Sophia, answer me this very minute!"

"A branch hit my head."

"That is all we need. Is it bleeding?"

Sophia felt her forehead, "Yes."

"Keep talking and put your hand out in front of you. I am coming for you."

"I thought you had an objection to my rambling?"

"Keep talking, *Sophia.*"

"I am over here and I really do not want you to move to the inn."

Rahzvon kept inching forward, sliding his feet. "Not to worry, I decided against it."

"Oh, Rahzvon, you have made me so happy," she spoke to the darkness before her.

"It is for the best, Phia. This way we can spend more time together before I leave. There would have been a great deal of time lost in traveling to the inn. Keep talking...Phia?"

"I am down here. *Leaving?* What do you mean—you are leaving? Where are you going?"

"I can see you now." A stream of starlight shone on her face. "Did you fall when you hit the branch?"

"*Where are you going,* Rahzvon?" Sophia demanded.

"Here let me help you up." He reached for her hand.

"I do not need your help. Why are you not answering me?"

"I am going home."

"Home! That witch Creaka shall have you burned at the stake!"

"*Creazna.* And I do not plan to storm the castle or tempt her army."

"When?" Sophia's spoke impatiently.

"No later than a fortnight. I shall come back, I promise you. I told you that I had to return home and claim that which is mine. I shan't have any peace until then."

"Well... then I am going with you."

"No...no, not this time. Do not ask me again."

Sophia knew that as much as she wanted to believe that Rahzvon was under her command, his tone demanded respect. The thought of him actually leaving her became unbearable. Rahzvon placed his hand under her chin and felt her tears falling to his hand.

"Phia, are you crying?" he said tenderly.

"Those are not tears, I am bleeding," she sniffled.

Rahzvon examined his fingers in the light. There was no blood.

"Come along, little one, or we shan't arrive at Brachney Hall before daybreak."

He reached for her hand. She refused it, but followed. Rahzvon soon felt the pulling of a passenger on his sleeve. He dropped his hand down and Sophia latched on to it, but only out of sheer necessity.

They reached the clearing where Brachney Hall loomed in the distance. The house was dark.

Rahzvon took her hands in his.

"Hopefully, everyone is sleeping. Now, remember, Heidi is in there. Be as quiet as possible. Do you still have the key, Phia?"

"Yes."

"No matter what happens with your uncle, I shall see you tomorrow, I promise." He leaned down and kissed her forehead. "Take care of that scratch as soon as you go in. Sleep well." He turned to leave.

"A damsel in distress cannot subsist on a light kiss on the forehead."

Rahzvon offered nothing more.

"I thought you were a *man*. I was mistaken."

"I am more than a man, I am a gentleman and a gentleman does not kiss a young lady in her night clothing. *Good night*, Phia. Until tomorrow, when you are donning proper attire," he gave her a promising grin and ran out toward the pasture.

Sophia returned his wave, and then pulled the key from her pocket. She rushed to the flagstone path and had no sooner stepped on it when her foot caught on a raised stone. She went flying forward, the key hurling from her hand to the grass. She lay there for a minute, and then sat up to examine her bleeding knees. She raised the hem of her tattered gown. *He is a mad man and I am a case for the infirmary.* She pushed herself to her feet, grimacing with the stinging of her scrapes.

The key, where is the key? She looked in every direction. "Oh, no!" *it fell in the grass!* She got down on her aching knees and began crawling around the areas near the path. Her fingers slid through the tall damp grass searching every inch. Several minutes later, she moved to the other side of the path to search.

"Lookin' for somethin'?"

Sophia turned with a start. "Oh, Tavy, it is you."

"Miss Muffet, what are ya doin' out here at this hour?"

"I might ask you the same?"

"Yer uncle gave me permission to fish the pond. It's o'er-stocked."

"Fishing, now?"

"I just walked in from the loch, missin' the sea, again... hae ye lost somethin'?"

"The key to the house—it flew out of my hand when I fell."

"I'll help ya look."

"Thank you, but it is hopeless."

"Knock on the door."

"Not at this hour."

"I can walk ye back home," Tavy offered.

"I am locked out of there, as well."

"I can take ya to the Dugans."

"Oh, definitely not. Mrs. Du–"

"I know, Ma Dugan is inclined to sharin' information."

Sophia laughed, "Indeed she is."

She looked toward the pasture. "I might as well go back to the barn and tell Rahzvon."

"A young lassie shoudna be walkin' alone. I'll walk wit' ya."

Sophia took three steps, stopped and groaned. "My knees are so bruised."

The brawny sailor immediately lifted her from the ground and started carrying her like sack of grain.

"Tavy, you need not trouble yourself, I am *not* light."

"Me pleasure, ye are like a tiny herrin' compared to the loaded nets I would be pullin'."

"Thank you," she relaxed, going limp.

"Rest, lassie." Tavy trudged through the pasture. When he reached the barn, he pulled the door open wider with the toe of his boot, revealing Rahzvon sitting on a bale, reading. Rahzvon dropped the book and flew to his feet when Tavy moved into the light with Sophia draped over his shoulder.

"Good evenin' gypsy." Tavy grinned. Sophia opened her eyes, turning to the dim light.

"Put her down, now, you filthy—" Rahzvon began as Sophia slid to the ground.

"Rahzvon, stop it. I fell on the flagstones and lost the key. My knees are bruised. Henry was *kind* enough to carry me, so that I did not have to walk."

"Get away from *her*, McTavish."

"Rahzvon, if *anything,* you should be grateful to Henry!"

Tavy gave a slight nod. "I shall be leavin' now, Miss Muffet, if yer certain ye shall be all right."

"I shall be fine. Thank you, Henry. I shall talk with you later."

"Aye," Tavy agreed and sauntered out of the barn.

Rahzvon stood, glaring at Sophia in her torn, soiled gown. Sophia shook her head in disgust.

"What did you *expect* me to believe, Sophia? Your clothes, filthy and torn..." He walked over and peered up at Hiram's window. The room was still dark. Rahzvon stood there for a minute more, then walked out of the barn into the night.

Sophia waited for his return and walked slowly over to the bale where he had been reading, picked up the book and held it up to the light. She opened the cover. At the top were words in script. Sophia squinted to read them.

For Mrs. Rahzvon Sierzik

Chapter XV

"The Lesson"

"Once only by the garden gate
Our lips we joined and parted.
I must fulfil an empty fate
And travel the uncharted."

—Robert Louis Stevenson

He is married? Sophia's breathing became rapid, her stomach began knotting, and her hands trembling. *He has a wife? A wife! Creaz...is it her?*

Sophia sat down on the bale, gripping the book with both hands, her anger intensifying.

Rahzvon reappeared in the doorway.

Sophia's intense expression sent a chill through his body as she moved in on him. He stared at the small white-clad figure before him, with the sense that she had become a stranger of whom he knew nothing. She raised the book and spoke with a tone uncharacteristic of the young woman he knew. It was not one of her usual anger or disappointment, but reminiscent of the princess, filled with hatred and revenge.

"You fraud. How dare you? I trusted you. I shared my family with you. You lied to me. You gave me hope and promises. You made a fool of me, you—"

"Sophia, *what* has happened?" he asked cautiously.

"Do not pretend to be ignorant with me! This!" She pounded the book into his chest. "This is what has happened—deny this!"

"Deny what? You are not making sense."

She ripped the cover from the book and threw the remainder to the ground.

"This *Mr.* Sierzik, this!" she tapped her finger against the condemning name.

Rahzvon stared at the cover with confusion.

"Do not take me for a fool, Rahzvon! I can read!"

Rahzvon looked at the cover, then to Sophia. He grabbed the book cover from her hand and threw it to her feet.

"You obviously, *cannot!*" His face was now flushed in the light of the flickering flames. He stormed over to the stall, pulled open the door, grabbed Hunter's mane and pulled himself to the horse's back. With one smack, Hunter shot through the door out into the night.

Sophia stood trembling, her teeth clenched. She looked down at the cover and stared at it as though it were a viper. *What did he mean? Could I have misread it? Maybe it was for his mother?* Then she remembered that his father's name was Gaelon. *I am so confused. Was it his grandmother's name? Was his grandfather named Rahzvon?* She could not think clearly. She reached down, afraid to touch the cover and squatted in the dirt next to it. She bit her lip and reached for it. It was laying face down, concealing the awful truth. She lifted it carefully from the dust and carried it like a dead rat by the tail. She walked into the light, closed her eyes and turned the cover over.

There it was, unchanged.

For Mrs. Rahzvon Sierzik

Sophia stared at the words. Her eyes slowly moved downward.

Her hand flew to her mouth and gasped as she dropped it to the ground.

"No, no. What have I done?"

She turned to see Rahzvon standing in the doorway, covered in mud.

"Satisfied?" Rahzvon rebuked.

Stunned, Sophia nodded.

He pulled his dampened handkerchief from his pocket and wiped the streak of blood from the side of her face. "Turn around," he said unbuttoning his shirt.

Sophia turned and faced the loft while Rahzvon removed his boots and dirty clothes before slipping on clean trousers, shirt and socks.

"You can turn around, now."

Sophia complied, seeing him replacing his boots and scrubbing the mud from them with a flour sack. Sophia carefully lifted the tattered book cover from the floor. Rahzvon passed by her, grabbing her hand and pulling her towards the door, leading her to believe that she was to be tossed out. However, Rahzvon never released his grip.

"Where are we going?" she asked trying to keep up with each painstaking step.

Slowed by her pace, Rahzvon stopped at the garden gate and lifted her to his arms. He carried her to the back door, stood her on the step and went back through the gate to the Zigmann cottage. Sophia watched inquisitively as he rapped on the door and a light appeared in the kitchen window. She saw Rahzvon speaking with someone. *Is he asking for the key?*

Rahzvon promptly left the cottage and returned to join Sophia at the door. He moved her aside, unlocked the door and walked in. He held the door for her, closed it, and wiped his feet. When he offered her his arm, Sophia tried to smile, but was at a loss as to what the near future held for her.

They walked to the end of the dark corridor where Rahzvon lit the hall table lamp and carried it to the archway of the parlor. They glanced at each other in awe of the destruction in the room. Simultaneously, they mentally questioned the possibility of their absence being responsible for the aftermath. After lighting the wall sconce and brushing away plaster bits from the divan, Rahzvon nervously offered Sophia a seat. Every aspect of the scene was unnatural—the condition of the room, the fact that it was after two o'clock in the morning, Sophia's apparel and Rahzvon's mysterious behavior. Rahzvon stood before her with an air of stoicism, seemingly, preparing to speak. Instead, he carried the lamp to the hall. Sophia listened, expecting to hear the backdoor close, until a feeling of impending doom fell upon her in hearing his footsteps ascending the stairs.

With each step closer to the second floor, Rahzvon's stomach churned with a fear of the unexpected. *It must be done. I have to keep going or I shan't have the strength to continue.* He placed his right foot on the final step. *I shall confess everything and protect her at all cost.*

In the parlor, Sophia sat petrified, feeling nauseous and confused. *Why is he going up there? Please God, do not let him waken my uncle? Does he not realize how angry he may be?*

The distant rapping was proof that this was one prayer that was not to be answered. She strained to hear the muffled conversation that followed, but there were very few words exchanged, none of which she could discern. With the sound of approaching boots, Sophia fidgeted with her gown, trying to make it presentable, despite the tears, soiled areas and blood stains from her knees. *Has he lost his senses? What shall Uncle Hiram think?*

Hiram arrived first. He stood at the entrance to the parlor, donning the same clothing that he wore earlier that evening, but looking quite unkempt. Rahzvon appeared directly behind him and returned the lamp to the table in the hall. For one special moment, with certain pride, Sophia observed her two favorite men in the world tall, strong and striking in appearance. Then reality hit.

Hiram stepped over to Sophia, looked at her gown, turned and lunged at Rahzvon, grabbing him by his collar and pinning him to the wall.

"No, Uncle!" Sophia screamed.

Rahzvon made no effort in his defense, although he shared Hiram's strength.

Under the pressure of Hiram's large hand pressing on his throat, Rahzvon choked out the words, "I...never harmed her."

Sophia pulled on Hiram's arm, "No, uncle, no!"

Hiram's crazed expression and powerful hold slowly eased. Hiram stepped back away from the shaken young man and turned to Sophia who stood trembling, with her hands tightly clasped on the little book cover. Disturbed by the familiar regret of giving way to his temper, Hiram stared at her with absolute contrition. He noticed the scratch on her forehead and blood from her knees.

"Sophia, what hap—are you injured badly?"

"No, Uncle Hiram. It looks much worse than it really is. I fell on my knees on the flagstones at..."

"Sit down." Hiram stepped over the rubble, walked over to the water pitcher on the table next to the window seat, and dampened his hand-kerchief. He handed it to Sophia and turned away, motioning for Rahzvon to do the same. The two men redirected their view while Sophia dabbed her knees and lowered the hem of her gown.

"Thank you, Uncle Hiram," she mumbled softly.

The two men turned and Sophia handed Hiram the cloth, which he disposed of in the dustbin.

Hiram paused in deep thought and ran his fingers through his tussled curls. He placed his hands behind his back, walked over to the window seat and looked out across the dark moors. The grandfather clock chimed on the half hour. It was now two-thirty. Rahzvon looked at Sophia and began mentally preparing his explanation. Sophia closed her eyes wishing that she were anywhere else in the world— preferably in her bed upstairs.

Hiram turned. "Have a seat, Rahzvon." Hiram raised a disapproving brow when Rahzvon boldly took his place next to Sophia on the divan.

Now being in closer proximity, Rahzvon could see the dark circles beneath Sophia's eyes and the fatigue in her pathetic expression. He wanted to pull her in next to him and comfort her, knowing that he had to say something in her behalf.

"Sir, your niece has been through a great deal these last few hours. With your permission, I would like to remain and speak with you, but I insist that she retire. Any discussion with her can surely wait a few more hours, after she has had some sleep."

"You insist?" Hiram scoffed.

"Yes, sir," Rahzvon replied unwavering.

Hiram walked over to his wilting niece and lifted her from the divan, stepped over the broken table pieces and carried her to the archway. He turned, "Rahzvon, remain here."

Rahzvon heard Sophia whisper the word "promise" and he gave a discreet nod. Although he had promised to see her the next day, it had already arrived and he honestly did not know if he could honor his obligation.

Rahzvon took two deep breaths, relieved that the first phase of his mission was complete—Sophia would not witness his discussion with her uncle. He stepped over to the vacant divan where Sophia had sat. A vision of the small ghostly figure clung to his memory while the final confrontation to defend her honor lurked before him.

Although Hiram's stature was not notably larger than Rahzvon's, his presence was grander by tenfold. Hiram moved in social circles of great power and wealth. The gentle, quiet man of few words in public, bore a reputation in commerce associated with intolerance and impatience, never complacency or indecision. Hiram's renown character directed Rahzvon to act accordingly—handling the Master with kid gloves and optimum attention to accurate word choice in addressing the events of the past hours. Clear thinking was of the utmost importance. But, not unlike Sophia, Rahzvon suffered from emotional drain and sleep deprivation. The vital wording of his planned explanation had become scrambled and distorted with the passing minutes. The disturbing surroundings further aggravated his situation in providing an atmosphere of potential adversity. Little did he know, his opponent, too, was exhausted from earlier events.

Hiram returned to find Rahzvon sitting next to the dark, empty fireplace. Rahzvon stared helplessly into the abyss feeling his strength and rationale diminishing quickly.

Hiram sat down in the chair across from him. Rahzvon's plan to confess every sordid detail of the evening seemed to have withered on the vine. He had thought it to be the honorable solution to the problem—the only solution. Now, Rahzvon knew that he was lacking the wherewithal to present his case with any cognizance. So, he sat silent, allowing the grilling to begin.

"Mr. Sierzik, you wakened me at this unnatural hour, you presented my niece in a horrific appearance and yet, you sit there without explanation."

"Sir, I have reviewed my involvement in the events that led up to this moment and I find there are not words for which to defend my behavior."

"That is unsatisfactory, continue."

Rahzvon shifted uneasily. "Sir, you offered us your blessing, provided that we honored your conditions. I ignored those conditions and asked Sophia to meet me in the barn."

"Why?"

"Why, sir? I am a man, she is a lovely woman."

"Go on."

"She found herself locked out of the house when she attempted to return."

"Why did she not rap on the door? The front door knocker would wake up the dead."

"She... I advised her against it. I offered to take her to Brachney Hall. Mrs. McDonnally had given me a key."

"Did you?"

"Did I what, sir?"

"Take her to my uncle's home?"

"As far as the woods."

"You left her to traverse the woods alone at this hour?"

"No...I took her into the woods."

"What happened in the woods, Rahzvon?"

"She fell, sir. A branch. She hit her head." Rahzvon pointed feebly to his temple.

"Then what happened?"

"We were on our way to Brachney Hall and
...I lost the key?"

"You *lost* the key to Edward's house?"

"Yes, sir."

"How did you lose it, Rahzvon?"

Perspiration formed on Rahzvon's brow. "I do
not know, sir?"

"Where did you go, after you discovered that
you lost the key?"

"I went back to the barn."

"Back to the barn?"

"Yes, sir."

"And Sophia? Where was she?"

Rahzvon anxiously rubbed the back of his
neck, without responding.

"Did you leave her outside of my uncle's
home, or in the woods?"

"No, sir."

"Then where?"

"I took her back to the barn with me...she did
not want to go, but I..." Rahzvon said pathetically.

"No more!" Hiram shouted.

*Sophia dressed in chainmail and armed with
the shield bearing the McDonnally crest stood before
Creazna at the castle entrance. The aged princess,
wearing a poorly designed, ill-fitting gown spoke
with venomous words.*

"Birreatra nifilatee!"

"What does that mean?" Sophia asked.

*"Translation: you may be young and
uncommonly beautiful, but you are no match for me
and my armies! Rahzvon's fate is sealed, he shall
die at dawn! I warned him not to return!"*

*Two sentries seized Sophia from behind,
Sophia tried to scream, but the words would not
come.*

Sophia sat up in bed, breathing hard and
shaking. *Only a dream,* she realized, grateful that
Rahzvon was safe from the clutches of the vengeful
princess, but not of her uncle's.

Sophia slipped out of bed, pulled on her robe
and crept downstairs. She heard the muffled sound
of her uncle's voice in the parlor. *Poor Rahzvon,* she
thought, tiptoeing past to the kitchen. She took a
seat at the table in near darkness. *God, please
grant Rahzvon mercy. How shall I ever forgive uncle
Hiram if he sends him away forever? I shan't ever let
him leave!* She moved to the cot in the maid's room
to wait.

Hiram got up, walked behind the chair and
gripped the back of it, facing Rahzvon like a
preacher at his pulpit, staring coldly at the beaten
young man.

"Rahzvon, years ago, in this very room, I
witnessed my father interview a young man
suspected of embezzling from the clan. The scene
was one I shan't forget as long as I live."

Rahzvon listened fearfully to Hiram's
account.

"It became so unbearable, I asked permission
to leave. My father refused me. This young man of
nearly your same age offered responses to every
question my father asked. With each inquiry, the
young man grew weary and exposed. He began to
sweat and squirm under the intense pressure."

Rahzvon looked nervously at the portrait of Hiram's father above the mantle and the pieces of glass strewn beneath it.

"When my father asked the final question, the young man refused to answer him. My father stood tall before him and *reprimanded* the young man for his false testimony, but *commended* him for protecting his father, who was the actual embezzler. Rahzvon, I ask you that same question. Would the account which you have presented to me, be truthful and accurate?"

Rahzvon lowered his head shamefully.

"No, sir."

Hiram let out a sigh. Then silence.

"Rahzvon, go back to the barn and get some rest... for the record, Sophia explained everything on the way to her room— quickly, but in detail. I apologize for...for losing my temper," he said, eyeing the destruction.

Hiram walked to the archway, turned to Rahzvon and shook his finger at him.

"It is to your good fortune, lad, that I know that you are a man of honor and you...you are absolutely correct... a gentleman would not kiss a young lady in her night clothing."

Hiram gave an understanding, yet tired smile and went upstairs to retire.

Rahzvon collapsed deep into the overstuffed chair and closed his eyes. *Thank you.*

Hiram removed his shirt and tossed it on the chair. *I did not enjoy that discussion...but the lad needed to learn a lesson.* Hiram looked up and spoke with pride. "Gaelon, I shall do my best to advise your son. He is green, but a tribute to the Sierzik clan." Hiram walked over to the window and looked toward the barn.

Rahzvon blew out the lamps in the parlor and walked wearily down the hall to the back door. He opened it and entered the garden. Just before he reached the gate, he heard the calling of his name.

"Rahzvon!"

He turned around to see Sophia rushing towards him, holding the hem of her, fresh, white night dress. Above them, Hiram watched in disbelief.

At the first sight of Sophia, Rahzvon panicked and immediately ran to the pasture gate, opened and closed it, safely positioning himself on the opposite side. However, when Sophia climbed up to the second railing, Rahzvon could not refrain from stepping closer to place his hands over hers. Sophia's heart pounded, as she closed her eyes and leaned toward him.

Hiram looked away for only a second; his protective instincts drew him back.

Rahzvon smiled and moved his mouth close to Sophia's. She felt his breath as he whispered, "I love you, Phia."

Rahzvon's hands unconsciously slid through the gate to her waist. Hiram scowled, then smiled when Rahzvon quickly withdrew them and placed them back on the gate railing. The fervent kiss that followed, seared Hiram's already broken heart. He sat down on the bed, feeling deprived of that coveted aspect of life; the *love* was painfully gone.

Several minutes later, he heard Sophia's footsteps ascending the stairs and the closing of her bedroom door. Relieved that she had returned, he reached over to the starlit photograph of her standing next to him at the Tower of London.

"You are all that I have left, Sophia."

Looking toward the window, pondering, he ran his other hand across his chin.

"*Lord*, I am going to need all the help you can spare, for it is going to be a *very long* summer."

In the bedchamber down the hall, Sophia blew a kiss toward the barn and then held the red, tattered book cover up to the light. She proudly read it, one last time before retiring.

For Mrs. Rahzvon Sierzik

And at the bottom of the page:

I shall love you always, Phia.

Rahzvon

"She smiled and smiled—there was no hint
Of sadness in her face.
She held her gown on either side
To let her slippers show,
And up the walk she went with pride,
The way great ladies go."

—Edna St. Vincent Millay

Non-fictional facts referenced in Blessed Petals

Scottish Keys on cover—18th, 19th century
Zane Grey's novel *Riders of the Purple Sage*
Sherlock Holmes
Percheron and Hannoverian Horses
Manchester, Deeside, Newcastle (England)
Assassination of the editor of Newspaper Figaro (by wife of French Finance Minister)
Shaw's Pygmalion first showing in Venice

Scottish wedding traditions:
covering groom with soot, parading groom through street, groom carrying stone filled creel basket, friends washing bride's feet and search for ring, marriage banns, tying of bride and groom clan tartans, bride wearing something (old, new, borrowed, blue), pricking bride's finger for good luck and avoiding mirror on wedding day, bride to step out of house with right foot, grey horse for wedding carriage, bagpipe welcome at church, binding hands with tartan cloth, Celtic knotted ring, bride presented with tartan sash and clan pin, tossing of petal and silver coins, first dance, Auld Lang Syne sung by guests encircling couple, tiered wedding cake, Luckenbooth pin

German Volkszither
Oliver W. Holmes *Birthday Book* citation
Wind in the Willows by Kenneth Grahame
Ralph Waldo Emerson- essayist and poet
H.G. Wells' novel *The Time Machine*

Poetry Excerpts from the Chapters

Acknowledgements

Chronicle of the 20th Century.
New York: Chronicle Publications, 1987

Grun, Bernard. The Timetables of History: A
Horizontal Linkage of People and Events.
New York: Simon and Schuster, 1982.

Illustrated Encyclopedia of Scotland.
Anacortes,: Oyster Press, 2004.

Kidd, Dorothy. To See Ourselves. Edinburgh:
HarperCollins, 1992

Lacayo, Richard & Russell, George. Eyewitness
150 Years of Journalism. New York: Time Inc.
Magazine Company, 1995.

Summers, Gilbert. Exploring Rural Scotland.
Lincolnwood: Passport Books, 1996

Webster's International Encyclopedia. Naples:
Trident Press International, 1996.

Webster's New Biographical Dictionary.
Springfield: Merriam-Webster Inc, 1988.

Website for traditional wedding customs:
www.scotlandmusic.com

*I am a firm believer that education
should be an ongoing endeavor.
I stand by the unwritten law that education
should be entertaining for young and old, alike.
Thus, I incorporate
historic places, people, and events in my novels,
for your learning pleasure.*

*With loving thoughts,
Arianna Snow*